FELIX and CALCITE

#1 THE LAND OF THE TROLLS

Artur Laperla

Graphic Universe™ • Minneapolis

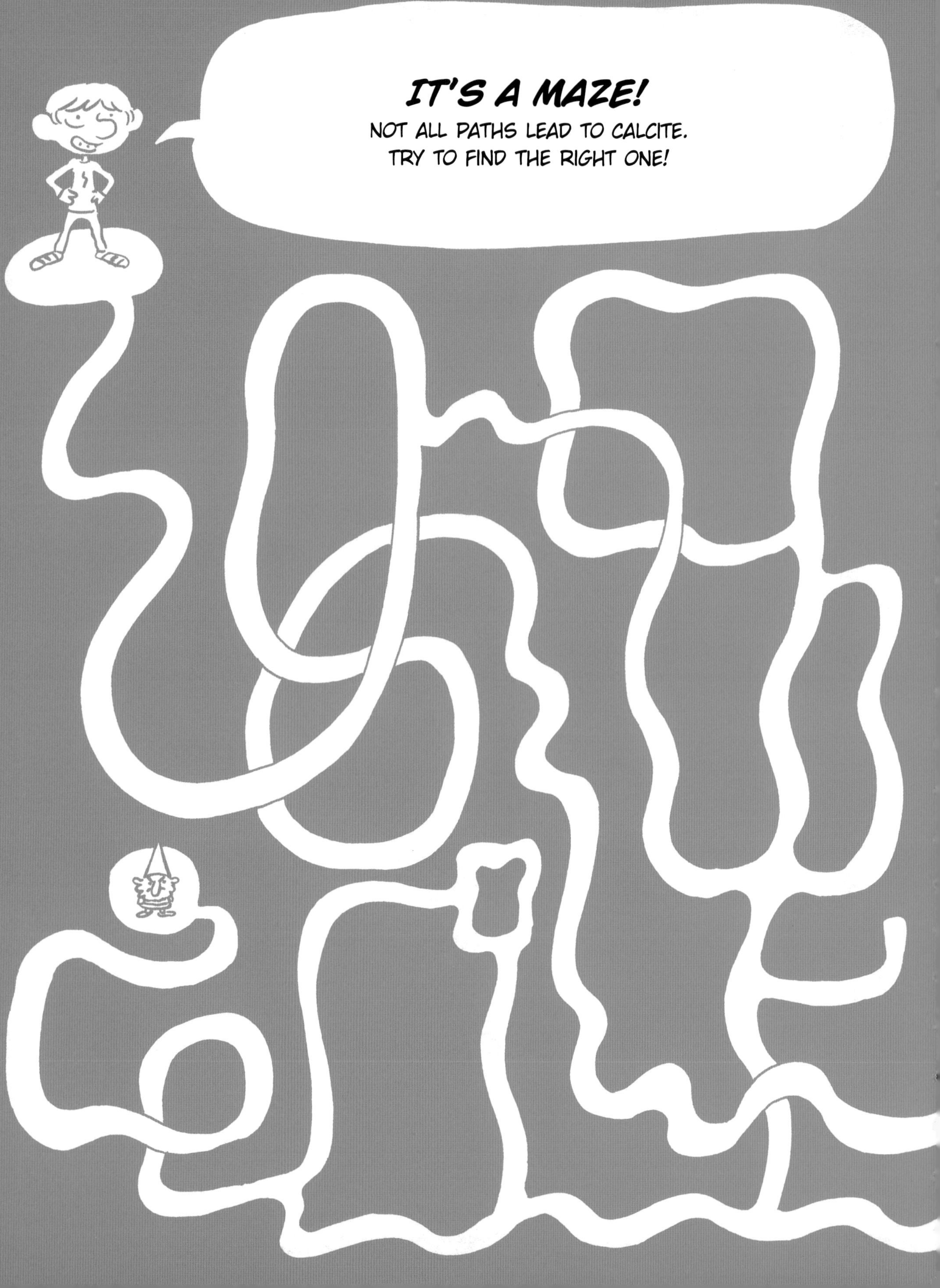
IT'S A MAZE!
NOT ALL PATHS LEAD TO CALCITE.
TRY TO FIND THE RIGHT ONE!

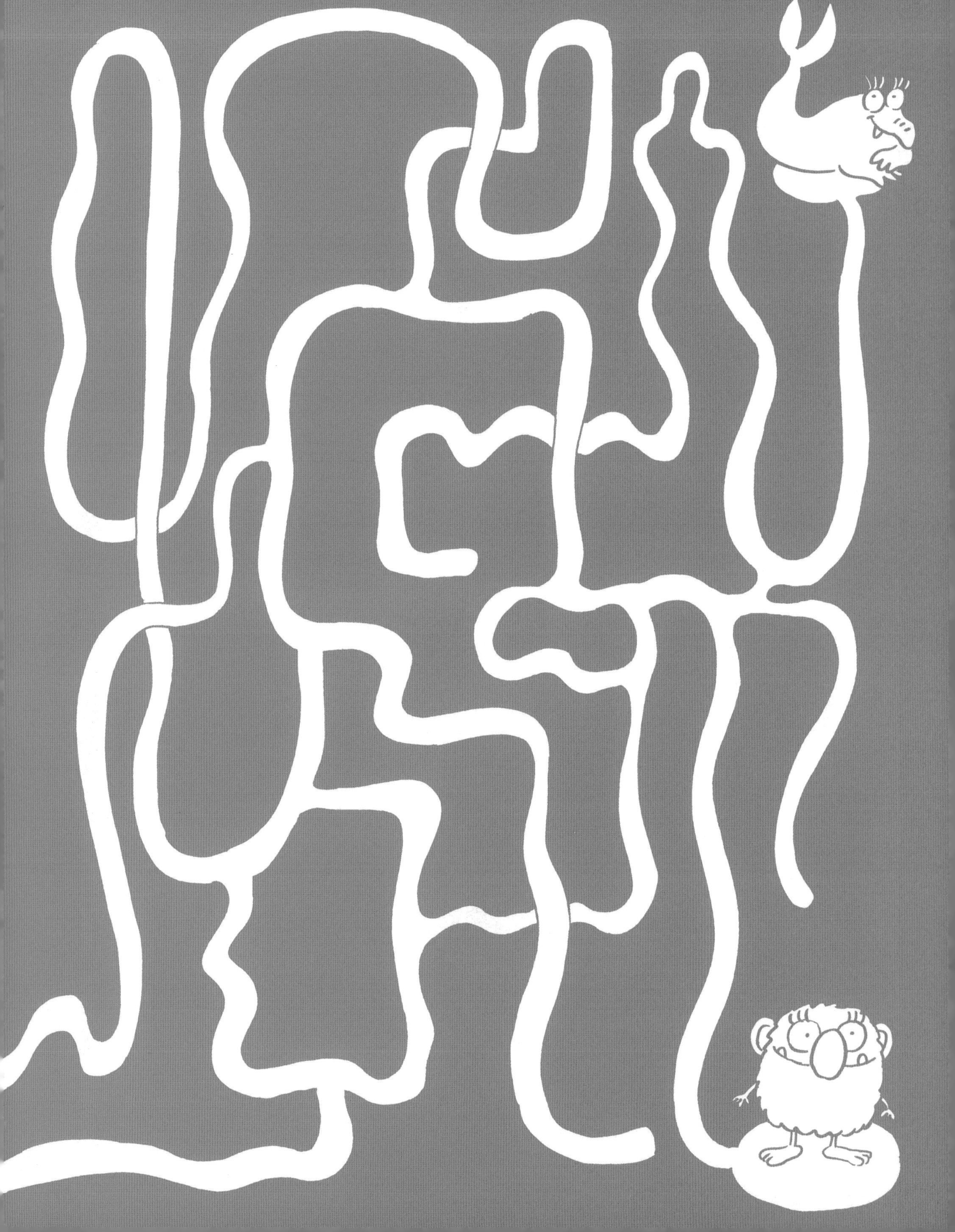

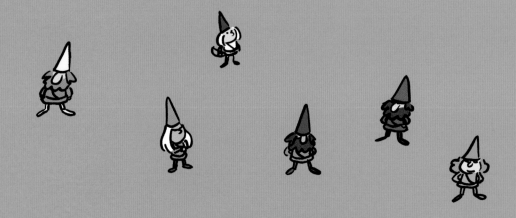

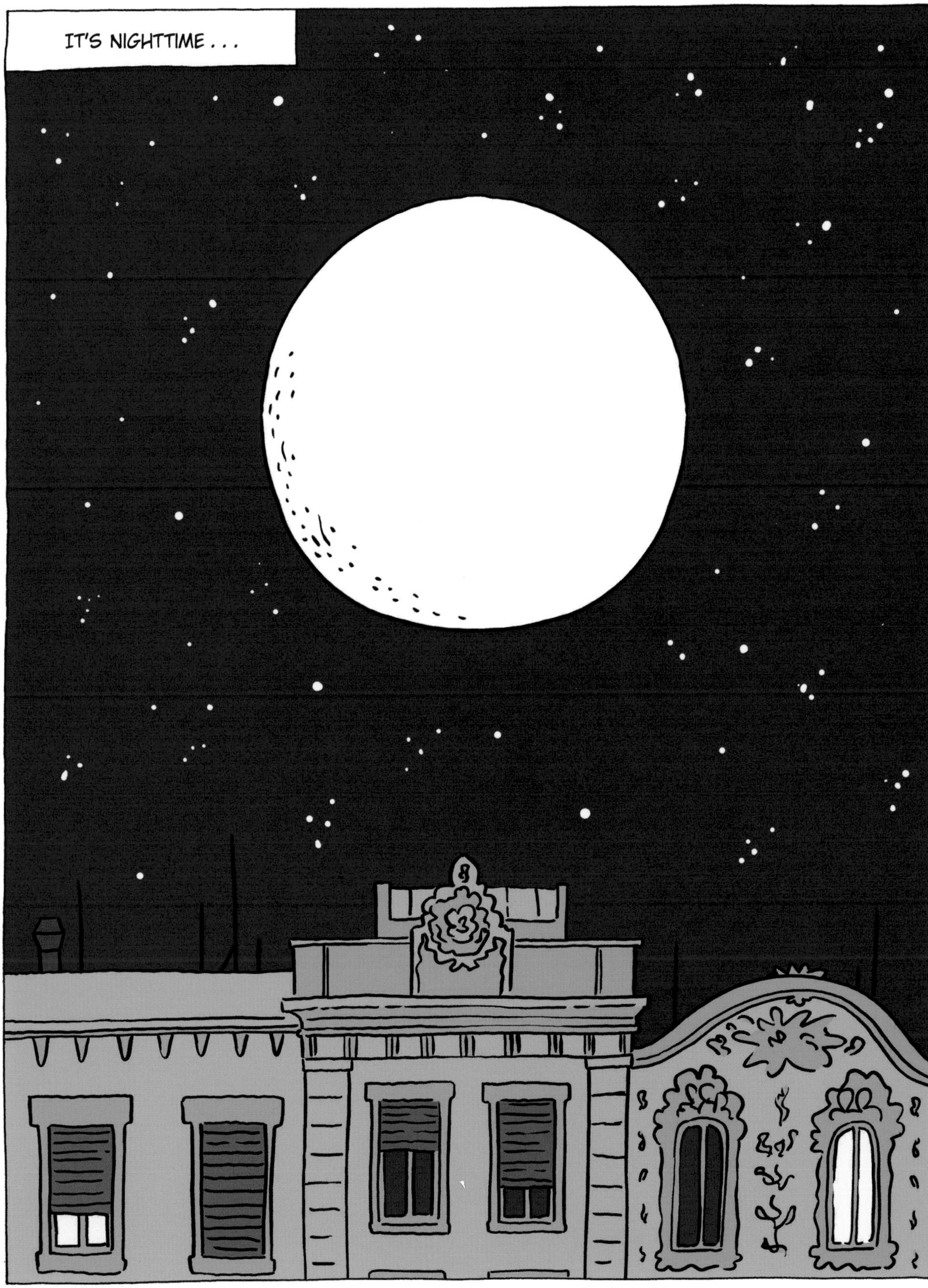
IT'S NIGHTTIME . . .

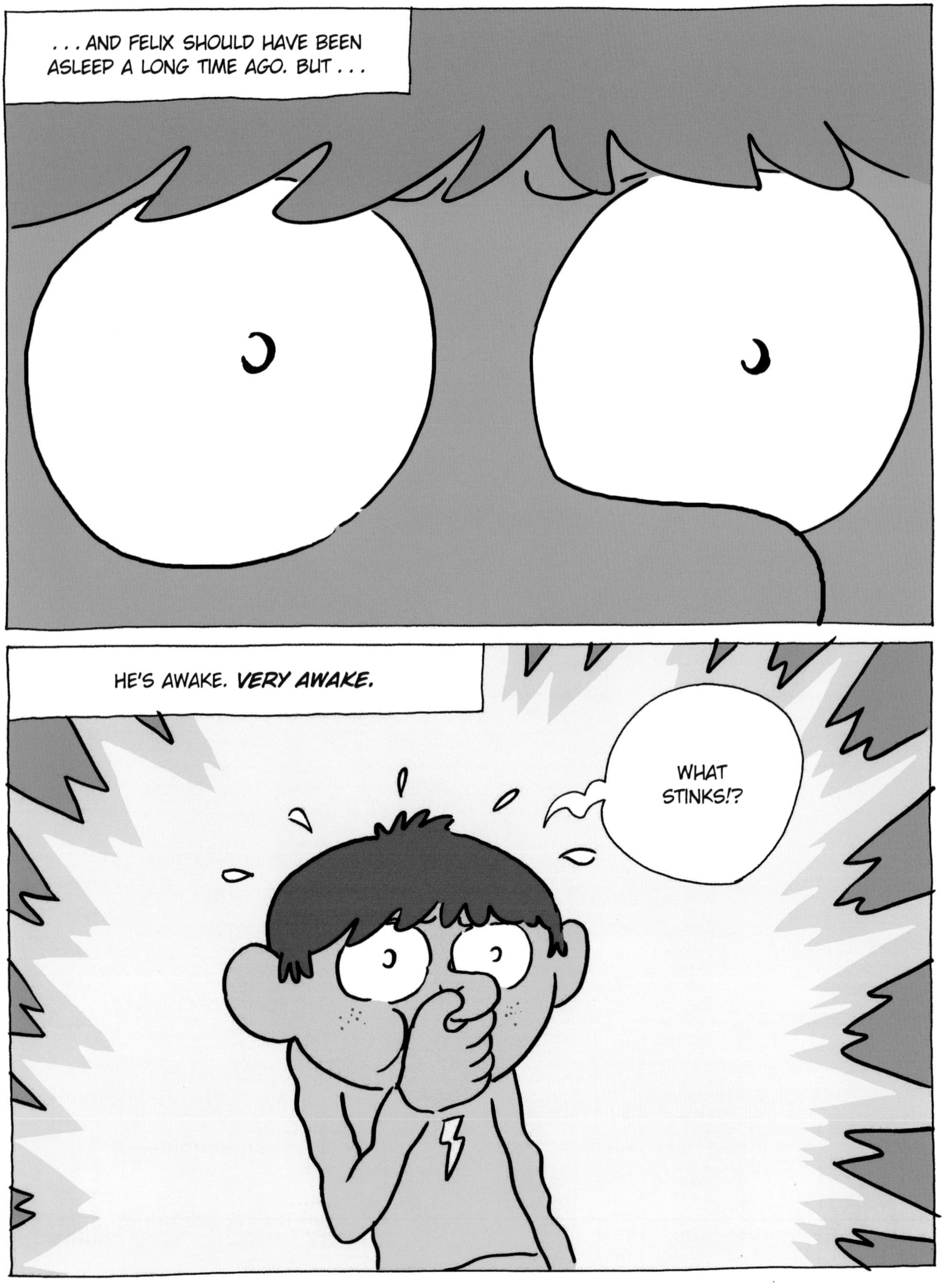
. . . AND FELIX SHOULD HAVE BEEN ASLEEP A LONG TIME AGO. BUT . . .
HE'S AWAKE. ***VERY AWAKE.***
WHAT STINKS!?

BECAUSE SOMEBODY JUST STUMBLED INTO HIS ROOM! IT LOOKS LIKE . . . A TROLL GIRL! A LITTLE TROLL GIRL!

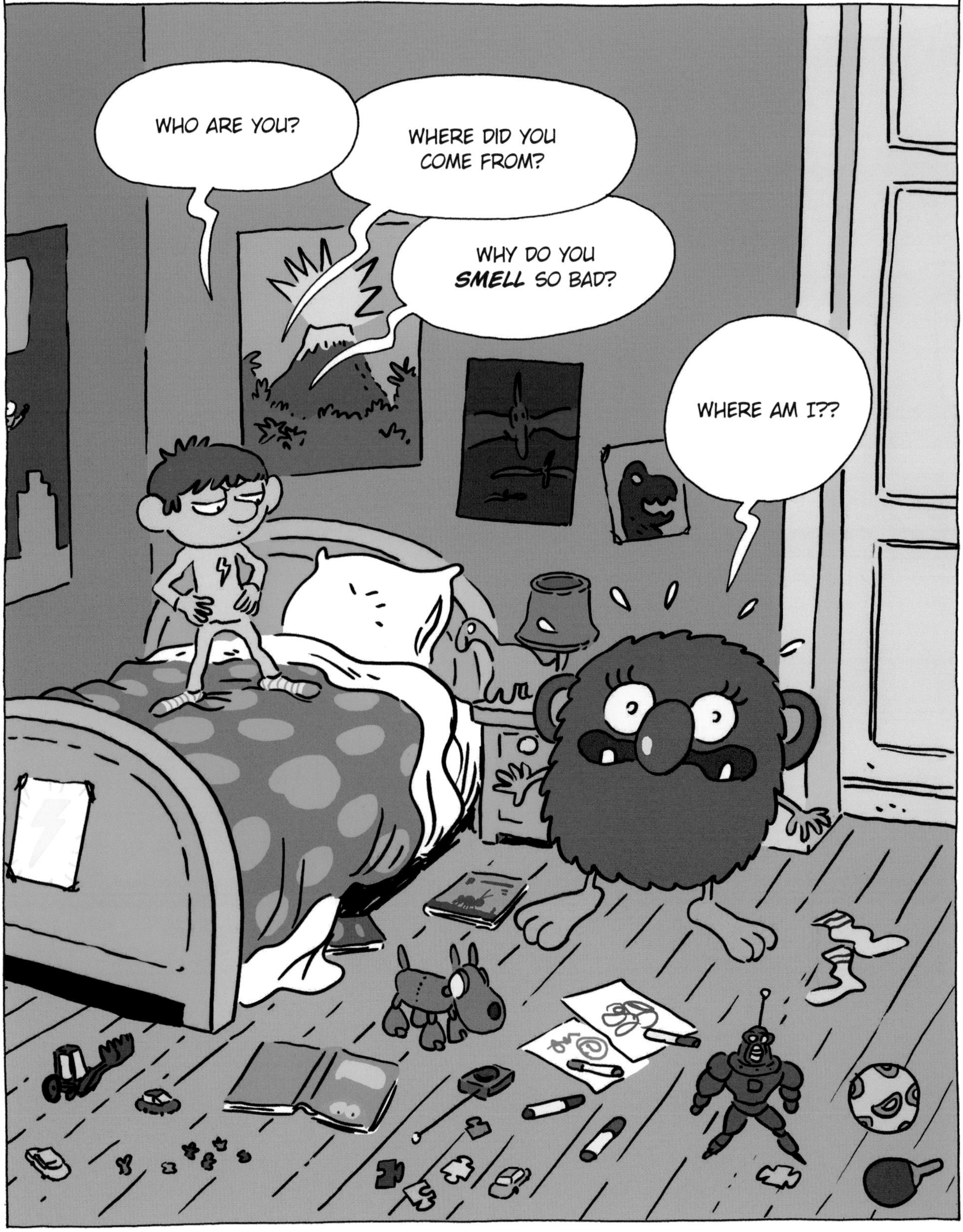

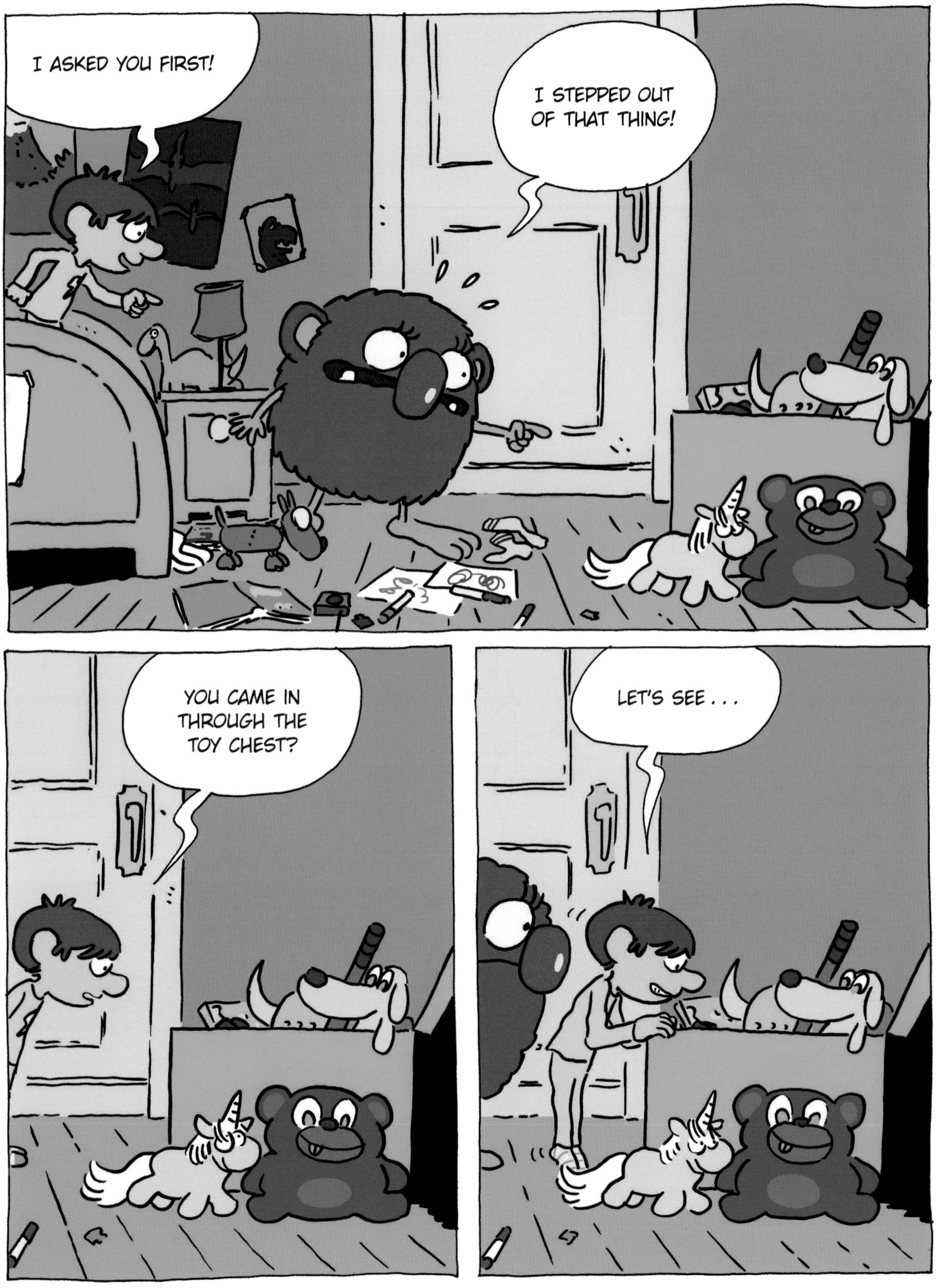
I ASKED YOU FIRST!
I STEPPED OUT OF THAT THING!
YOU CAME IN THROUGH THE TOY CHEST?
LET'S SEE . . .

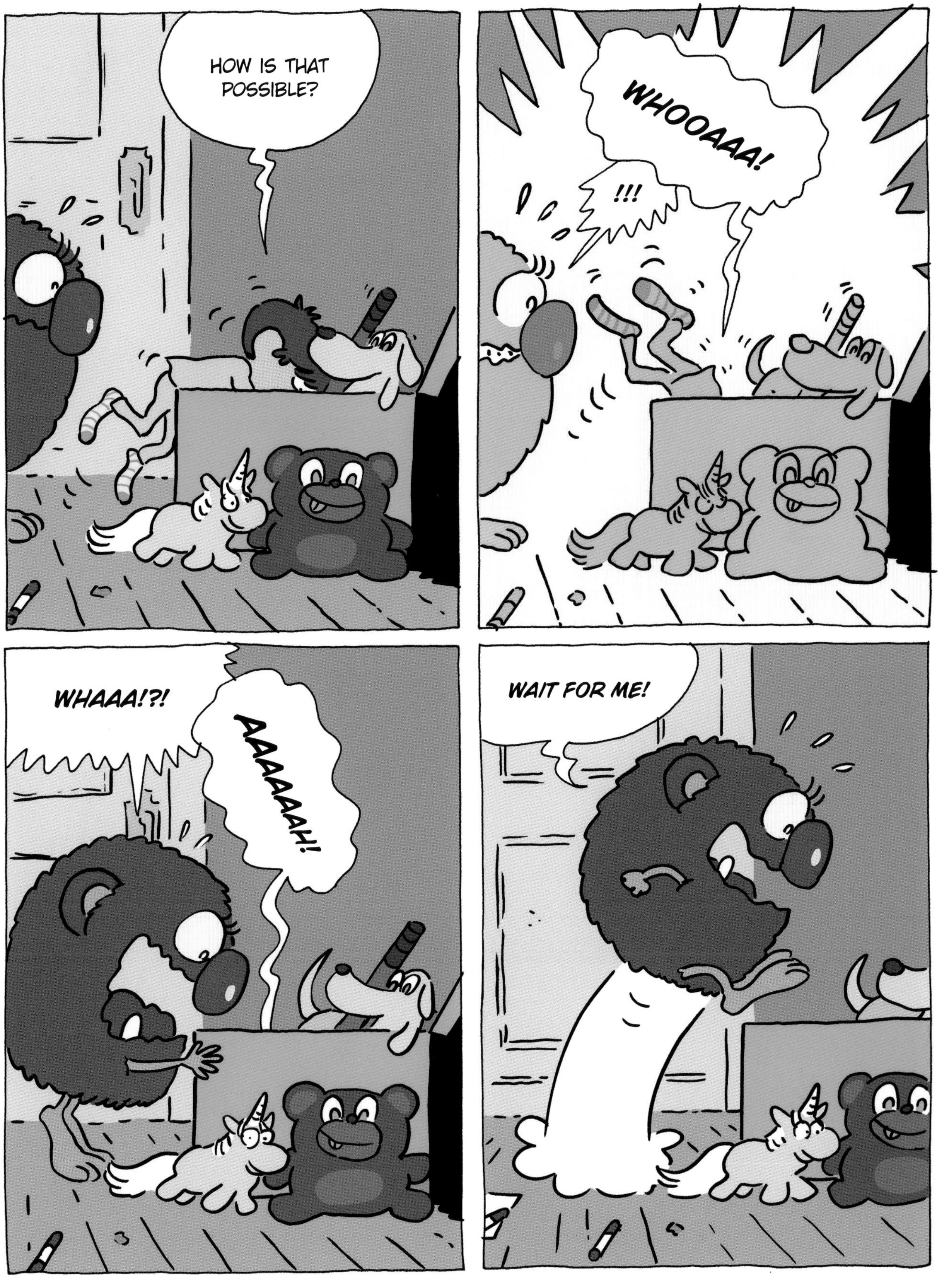
HOW IS THAT POSSIBLE?
WHOOAAA!
!!!
WHAAA!?!
AAAAAAAH!
WAIT FOR ME!

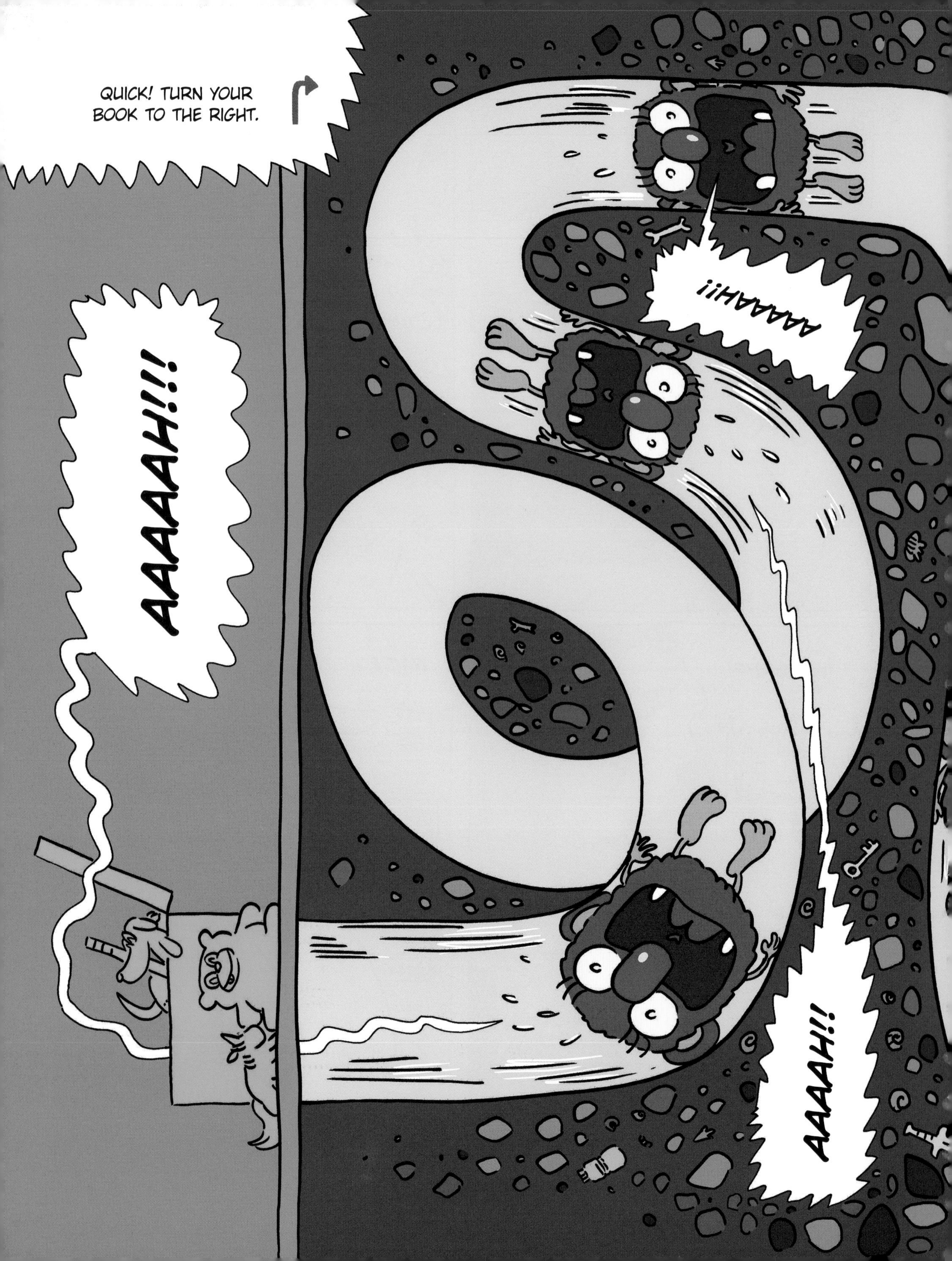
QUICK! TURN YOUR BOOK TO THE RIGHT.
AAAAAAH!!!!
AAAAH!!
AAAAAH!!

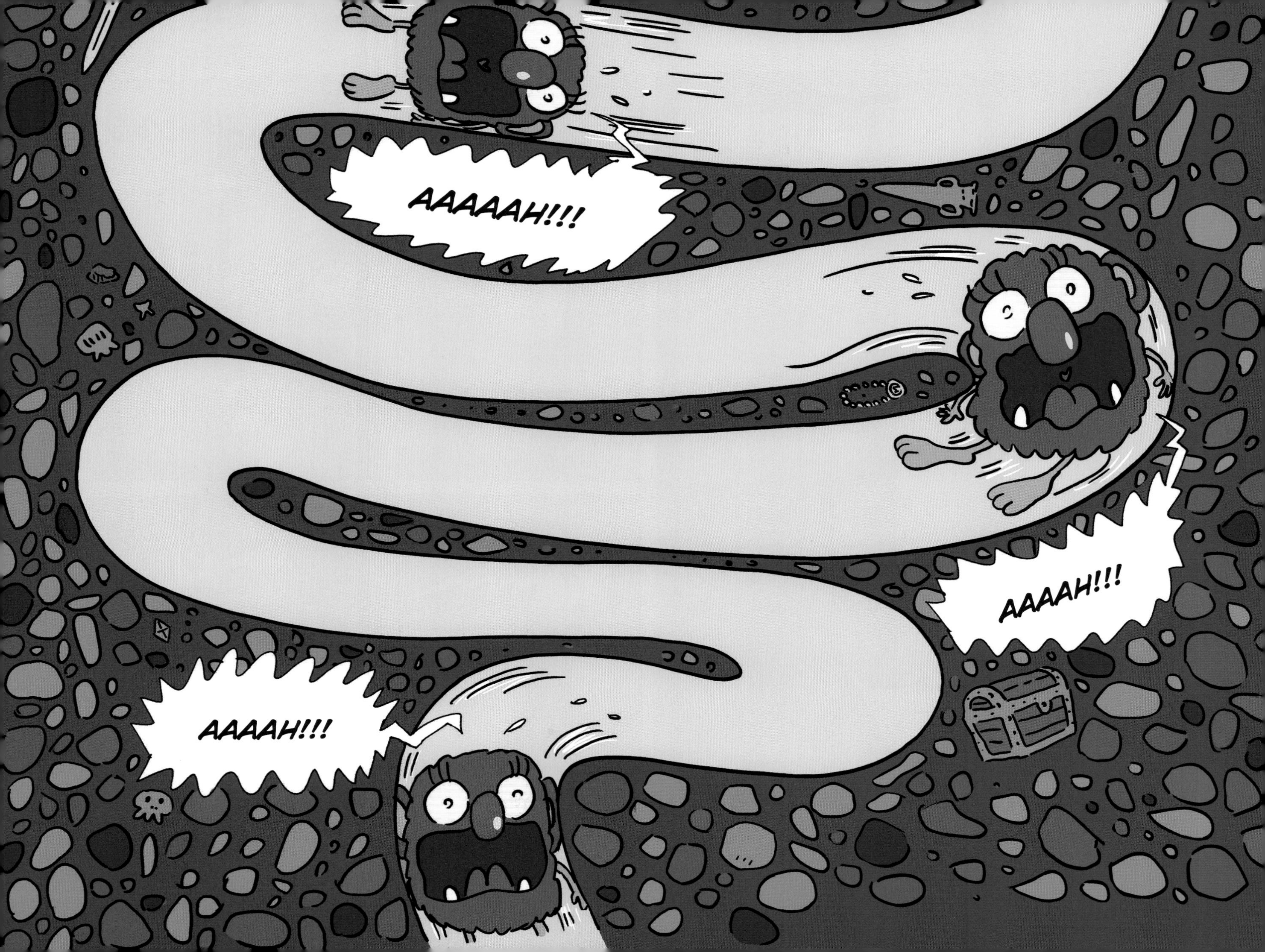
AAAAAH!!!
AAAAH!!!
AAAAH!!!

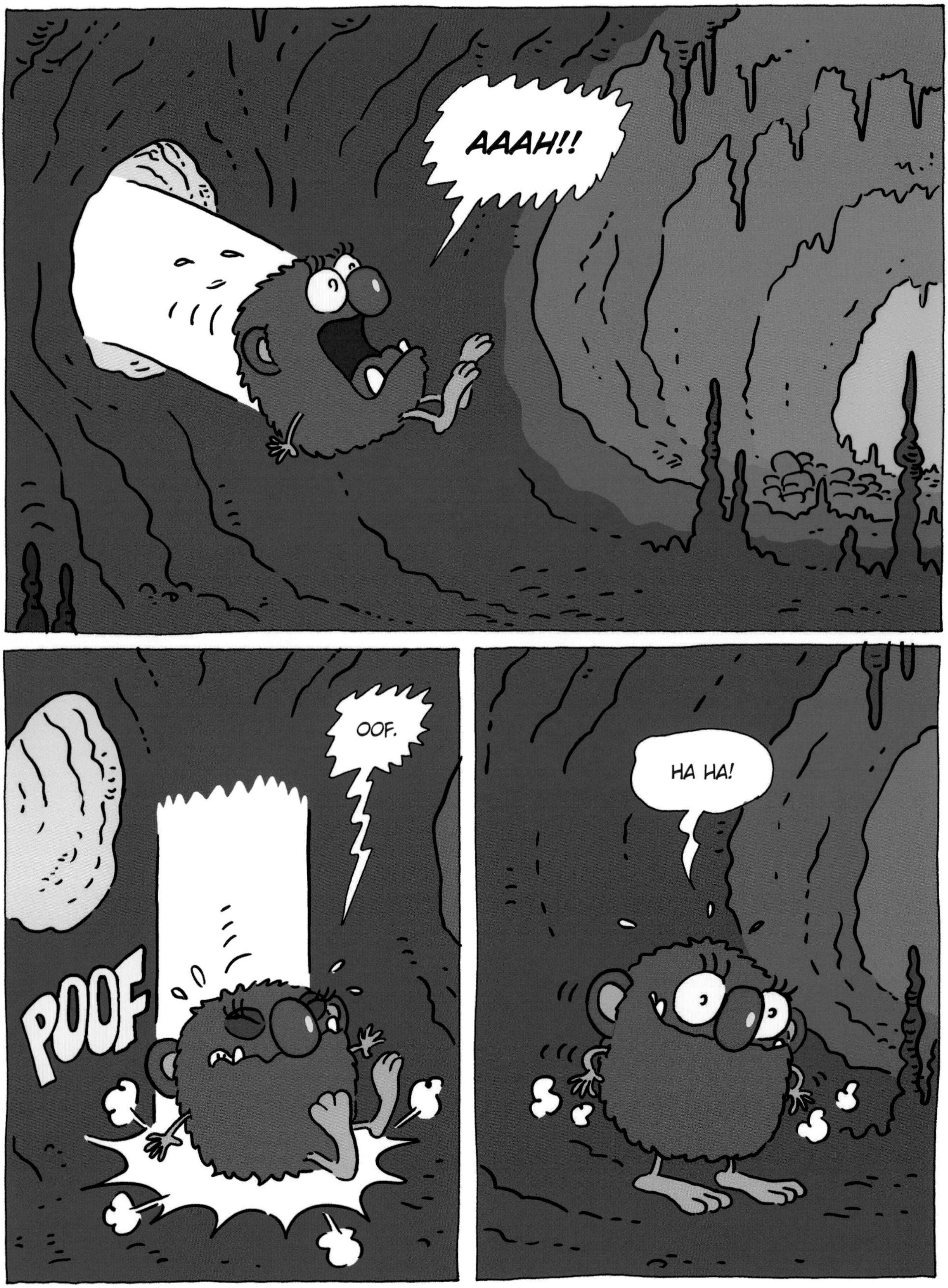
AAAH!!
POOF
OOF.
HA HA!

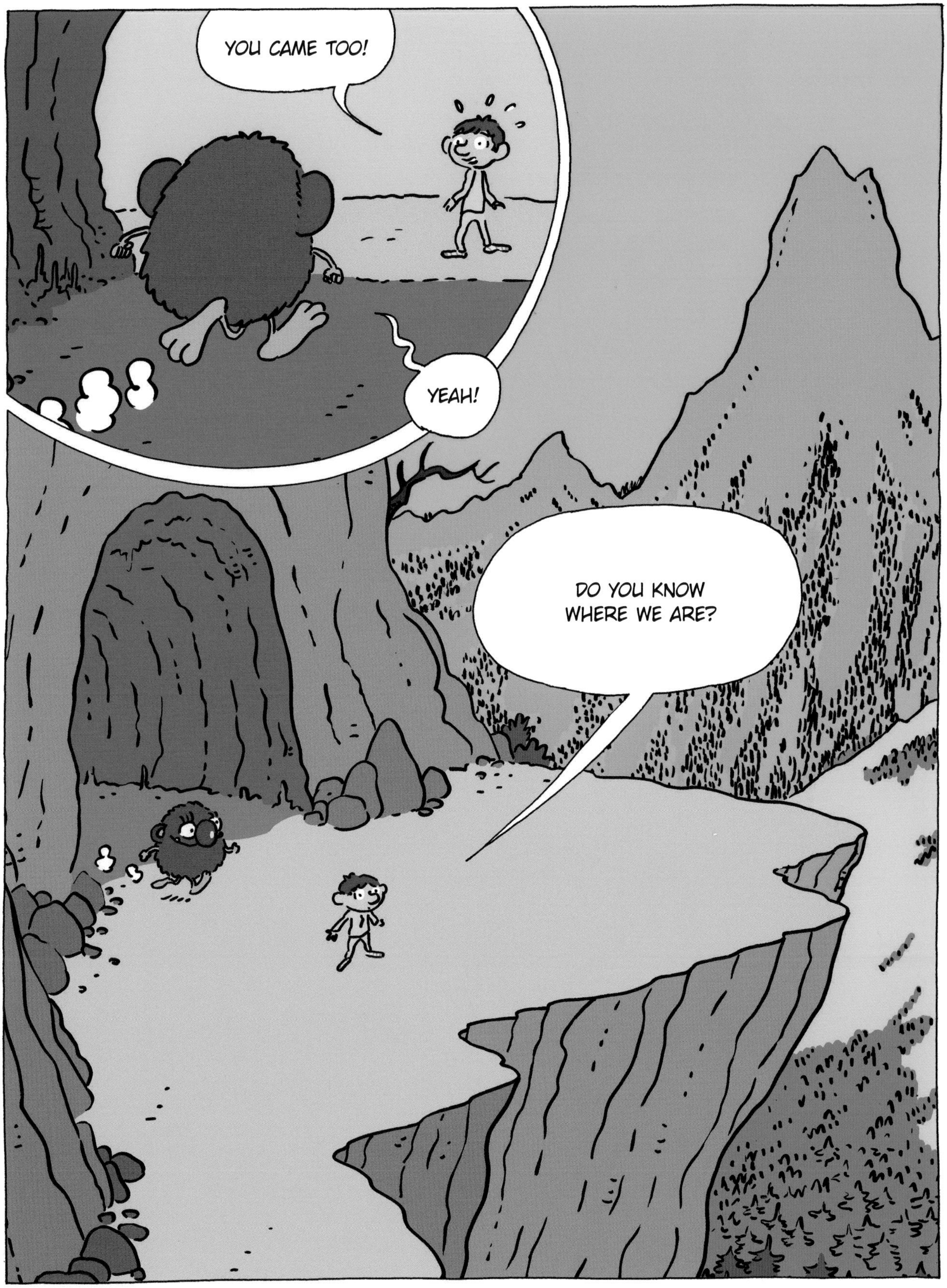
YOU CAME TOO!
YEAH!
DO YOU KNOW WHERE WE ARE?

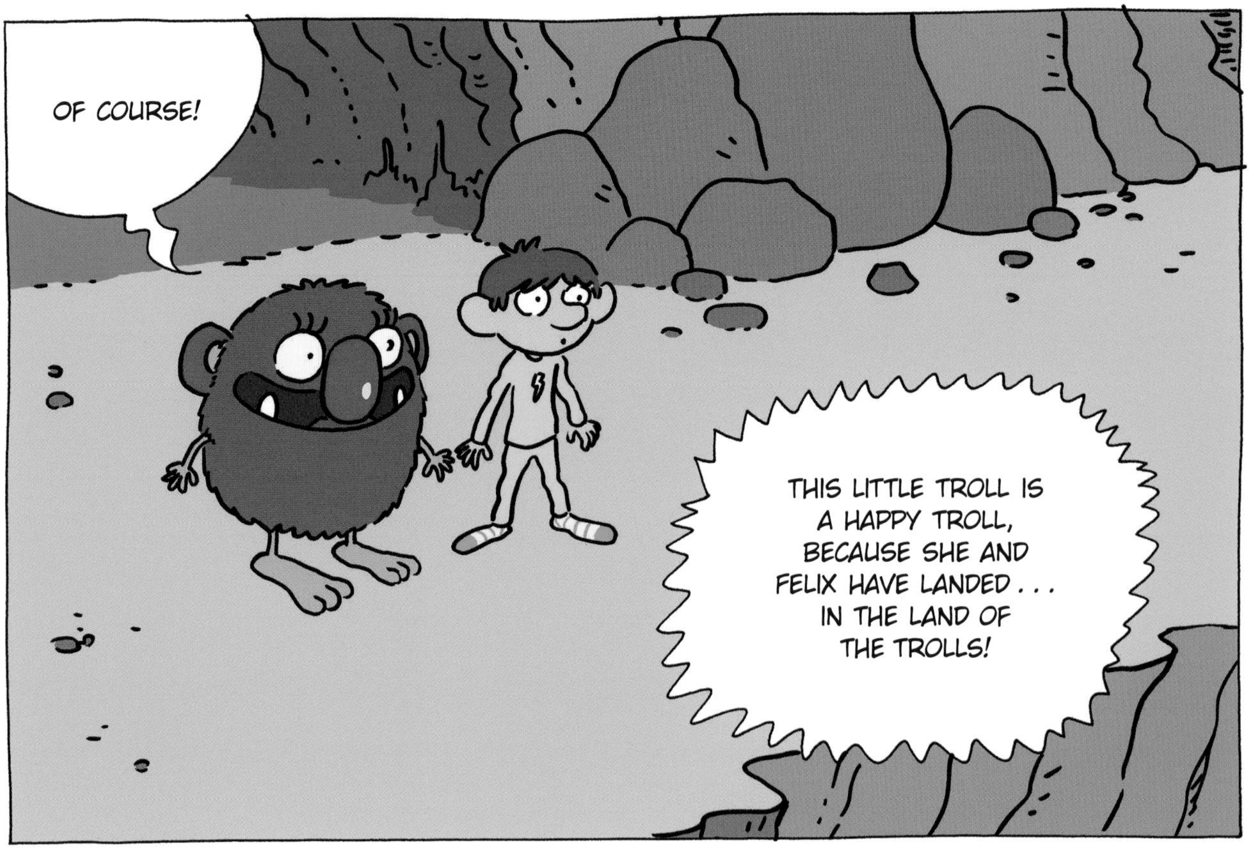
OF COURSE!
THIS LITTLE TROLL IS A HAPPY TROLL, BECAUSE SHE AND FELIX HAVE LANDED . . . IN THE LAND OF THE TROLLS!

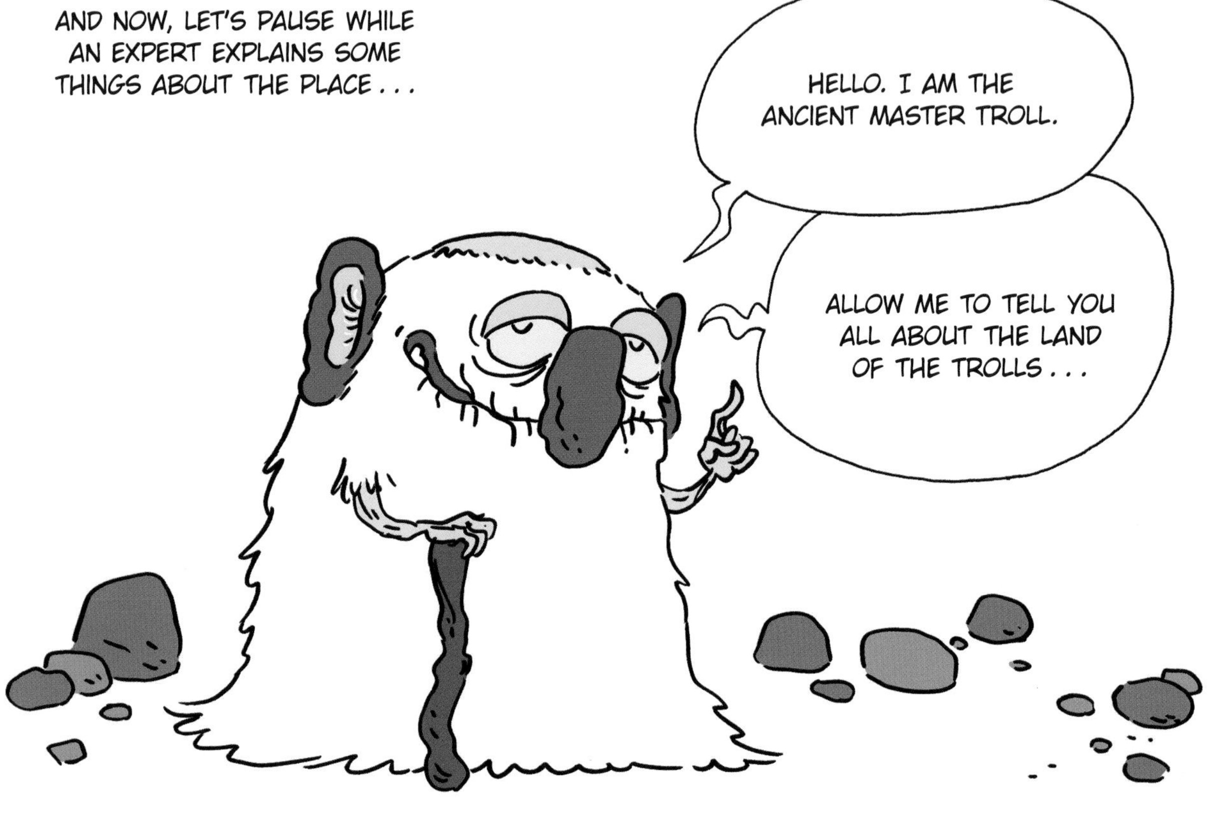
AND NOW, LET'S PAUSE WHILE AN EXPERT EXPLAINS SOME THINGS ABOUT THE PLACE . . .
HELLO. I AM THE ANCIENT MASTER TROLL.
ALLOW ME TO TELL YOU ALL ABOUT THE LAND OF THE TROLLS . . .

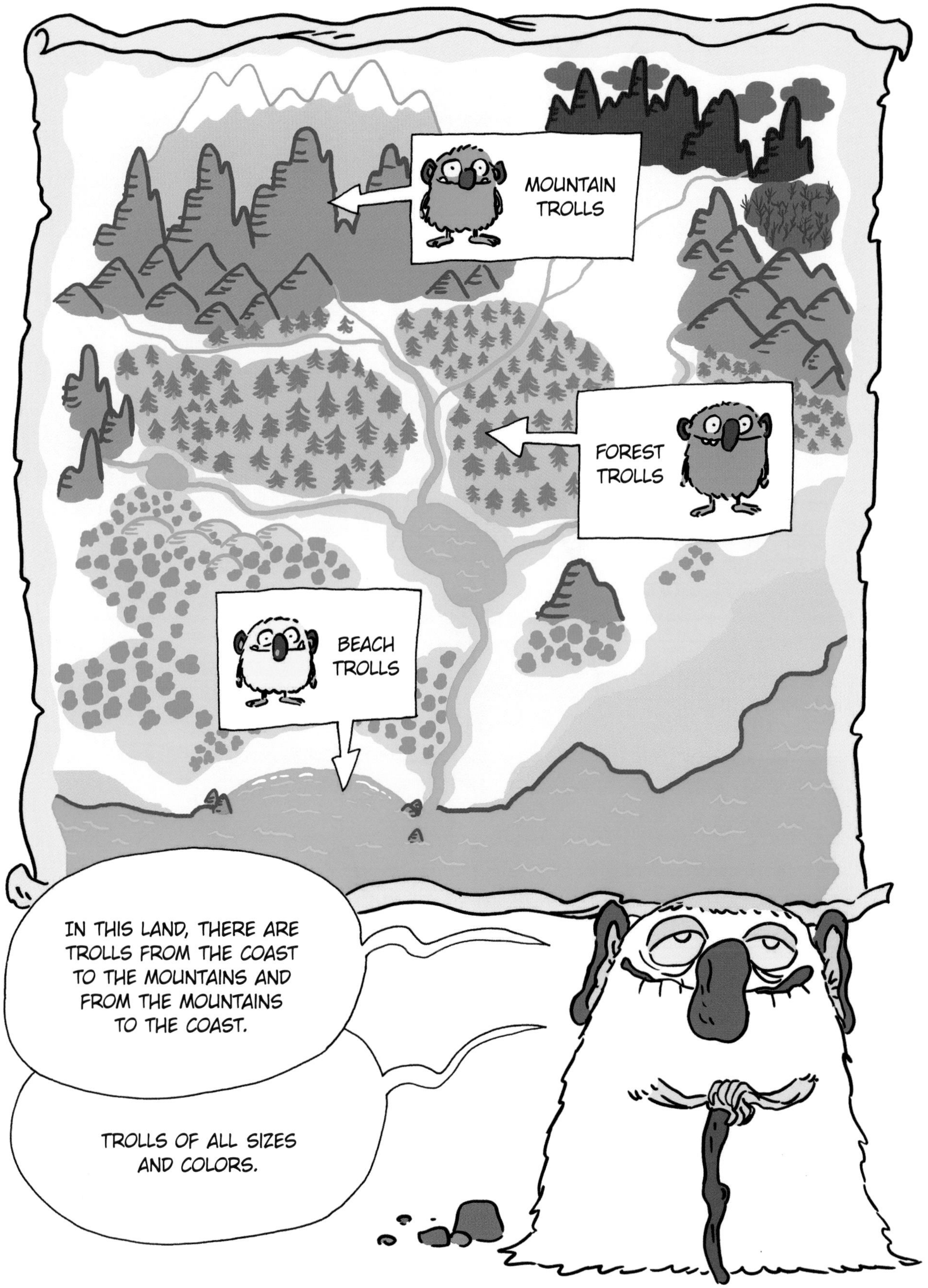
MOUNTAIN TROLLS
FOREST TROLLS
BEACH TROLLS
IN THIS LAND, THERE ARE TROLLS FROM THE COAST TO THE MOUNTAINS AND FROM THE MOUNTAINS TO THE COAST.
TROLLS OF ALL SIZES AND COLORS.

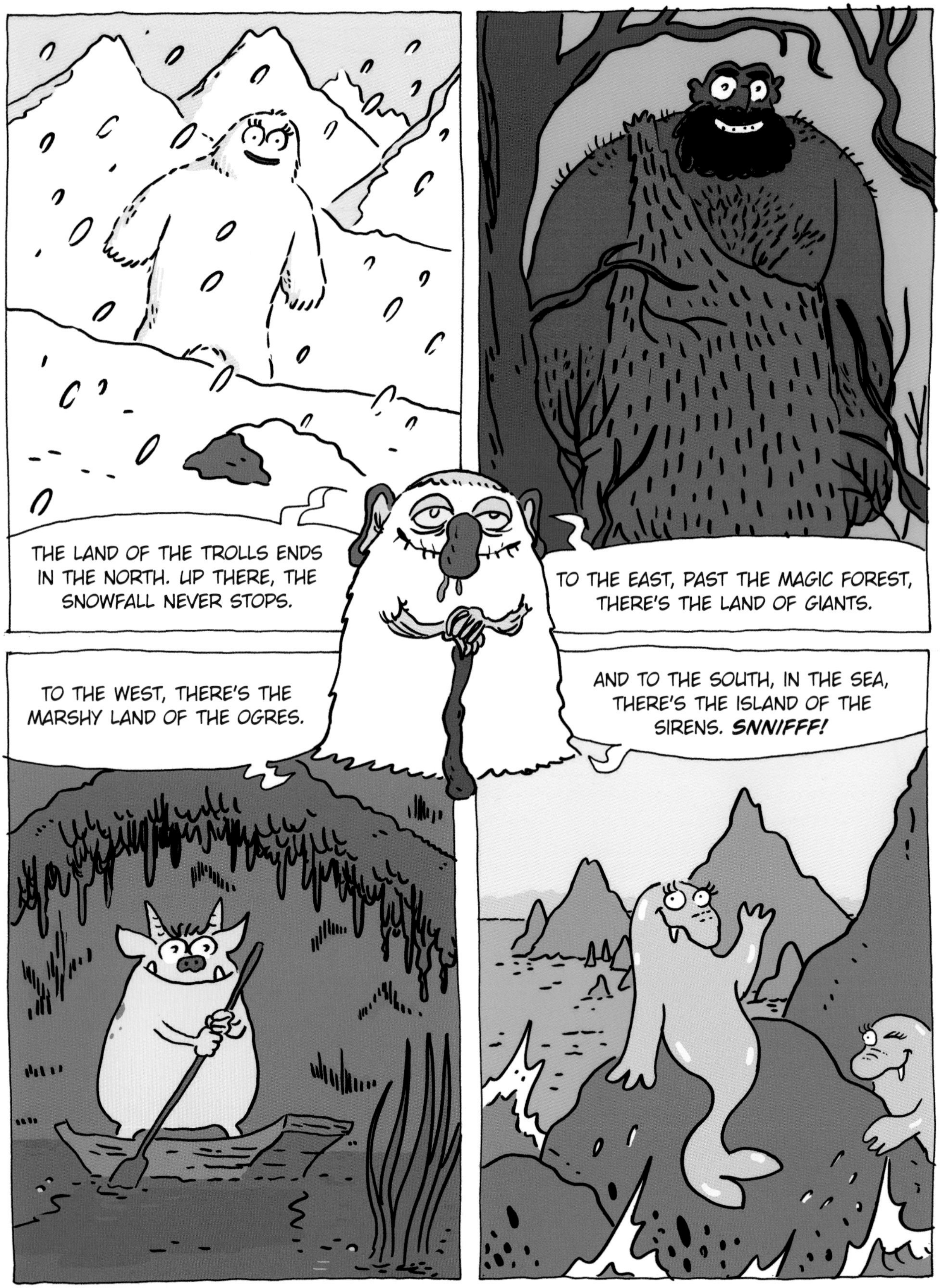
THE LAND OF THE TROLLS ENDS IN THE NORTH. UP THERE, THE SNOWFALL NEVER STOPS.
TO THE EAST, PAST THE MAGIC FOREST, THERE'S THE LAND OF GIANTS.
TO THE WEST, THERE'S THE MARSHY LAND OF THE OGRES.
AND TO THE SOUTH, IN THE SEA, THERE'S THE ISLAND OF THE SIRENS. SNNIFFF!

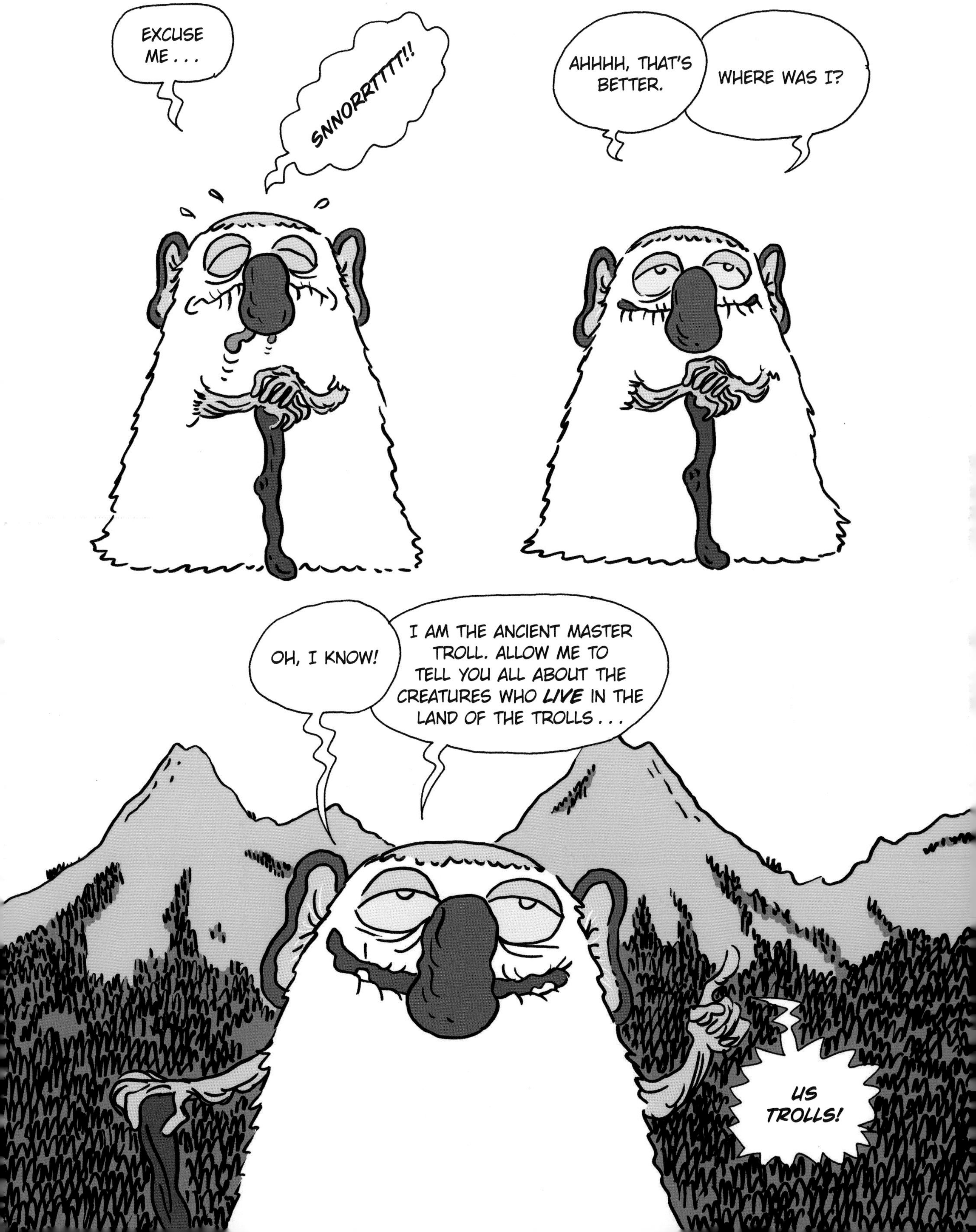
EXCUSE ME . . .
SNNORRTTTTT!!
AHHHH, THAT'S BETTER.
WHERE WAS I?
OH, I KNOW!
I AM THE ANCIENT MASTER TROLL. ALLOW ME TO TELL YOU ALL ABOUT THE CREATURES WHO LIVE IN THE LAND OF THE TROLLS . . .
US TROLLS!

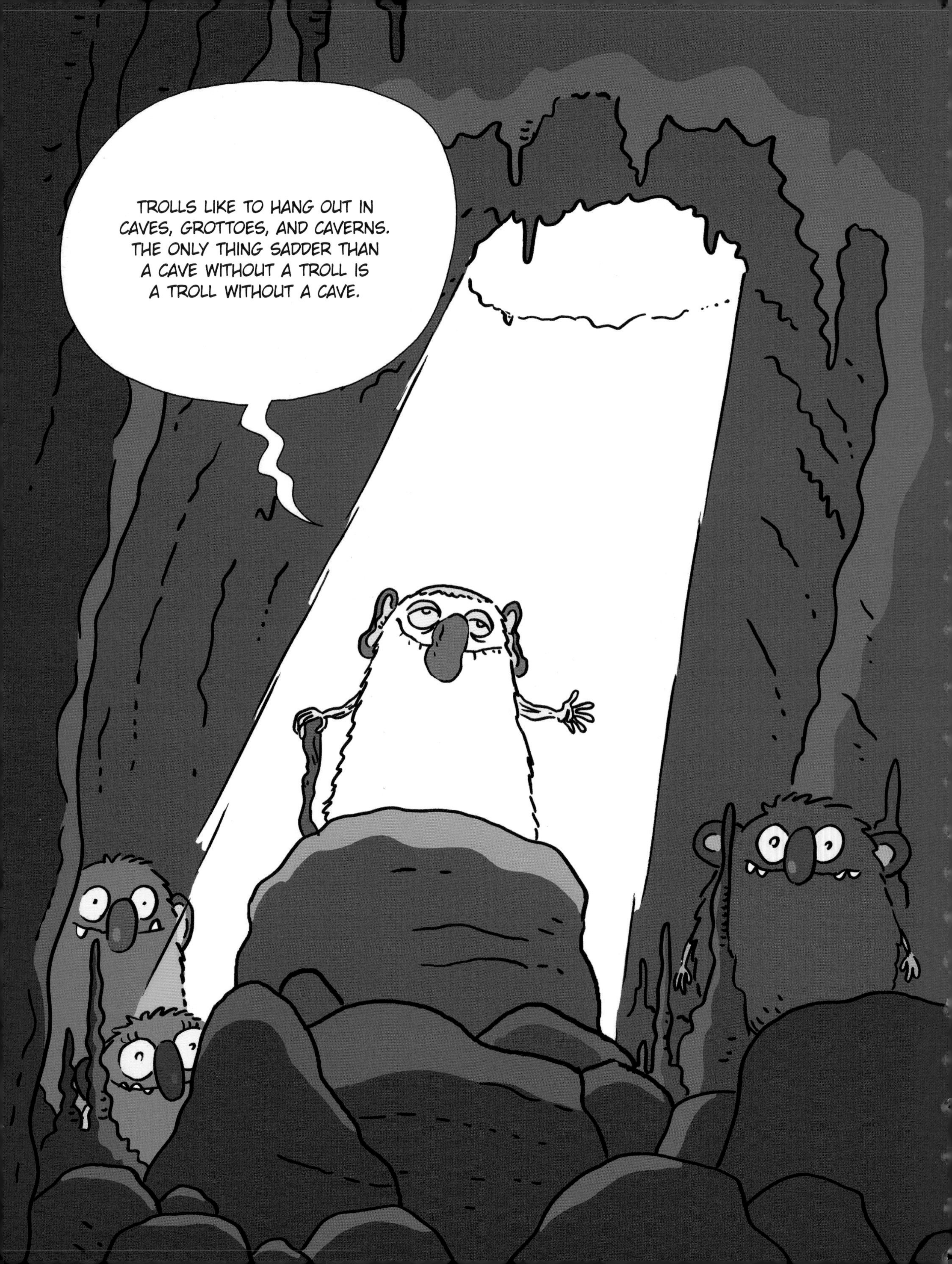
TROLLS LIKE TO HANG OUT IN CAVES, GROTTOES, AND CAVERNS. THE ONLY THING SADDER THAN A CAVE WITHOUT A TROLL IS A TROLL WITHOUT A CAVE.

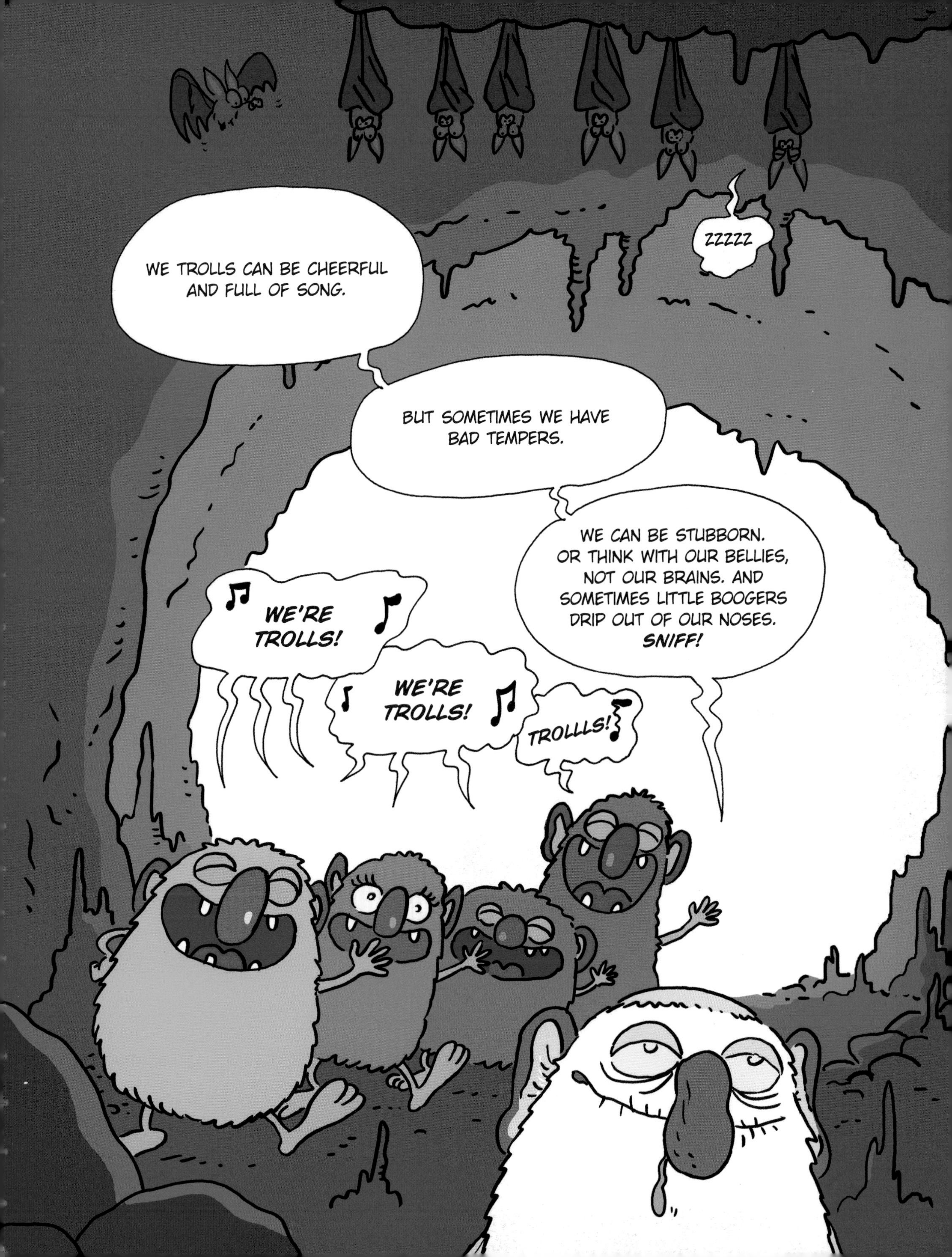

WE TROLLS CAN BE CHEERFUL AND FULL OF SONG.
ZZZZZ
BUT SOMETIMES WE HAVE BAD TEMPERS.
WE CAN BE STUBBORN. OR THINK WITH OUR BELLIES, NOT OUR BRAINS. AND SOMETIMES LITTLE BOOGERS DRIP OUT OF OUR NOSES. SNIFF!
WE'RE TROLLS!
WE'RE TROLLS!
TROLLLS!

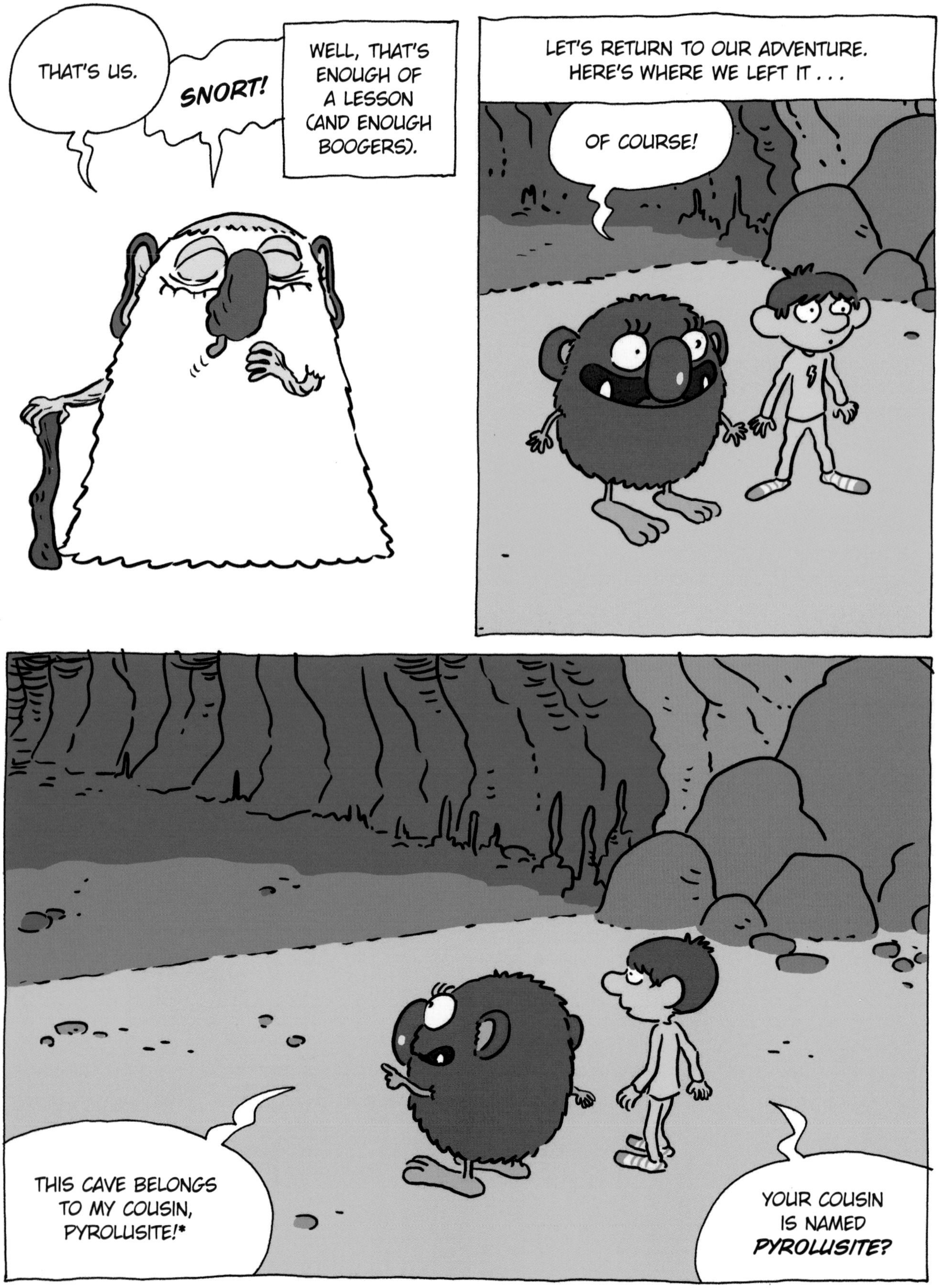
THAT'S US.
SNORT!
WELL, THAT'S ENOUGH OF A LESSON (AND ENOUGH BOOGERS).
LET'S RETURN TO OUR ADVENTURE. HERE'S WHERE WE LEFT IT . . .
OF COURSE!
THIS CAVE BELONGS TO MY COUSIN, PYROLUSITE!*
YOUR COUSIN IS NAMED **PYROLUSITE?**

*YOU CAN SAY THE NAME LIKE THIS: ***PIE-ROW-LOO-SITE!***

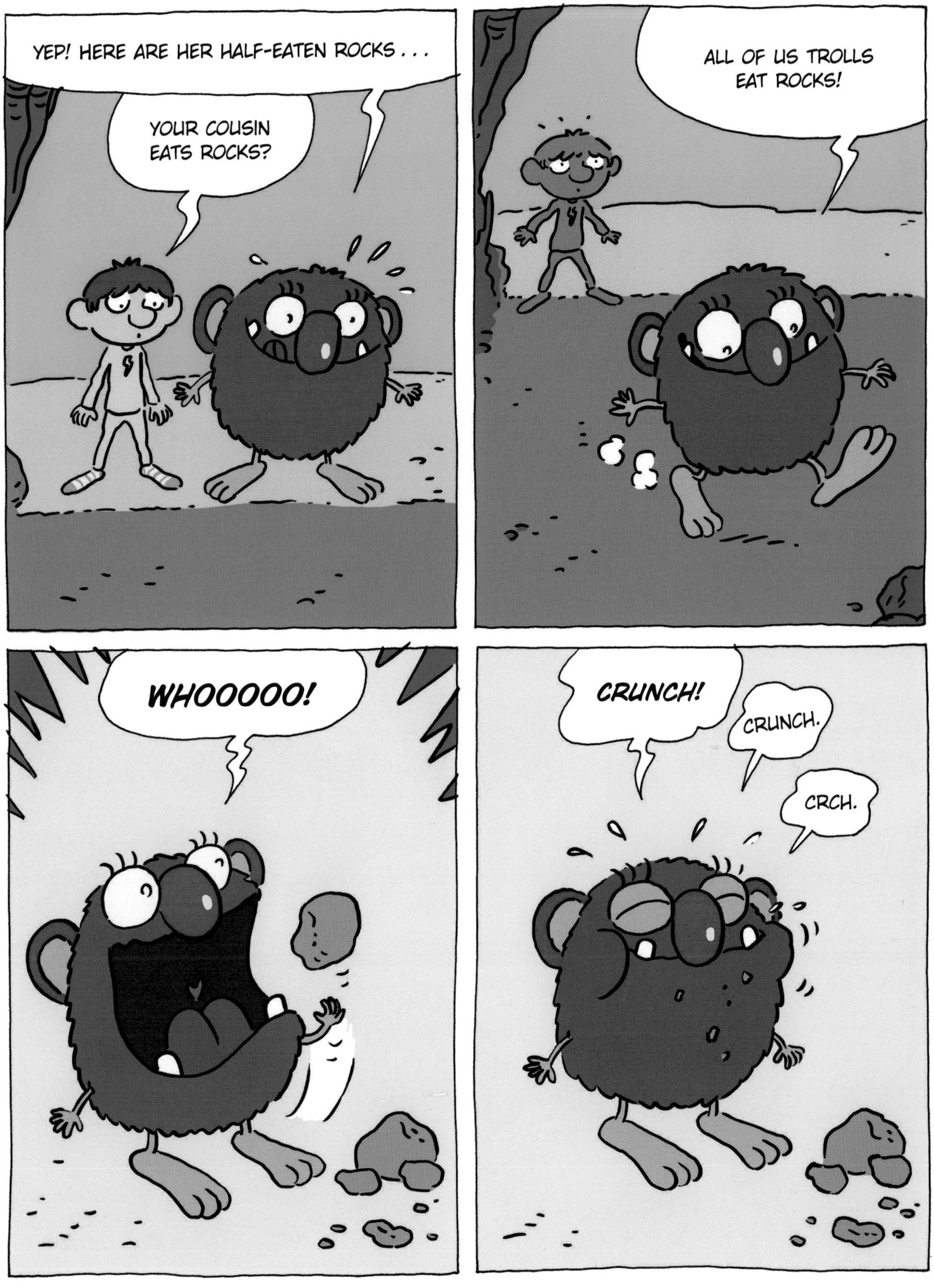
YEP! HERE ARE HER HALF-EATEN ROCKS . . .
YOUR COUSIN EATS ROCKS?
ALL OF US TROLLS EAT ROCKS!
WHOOOOO!
CRUNCH!
CRUNCH.
CRCH.

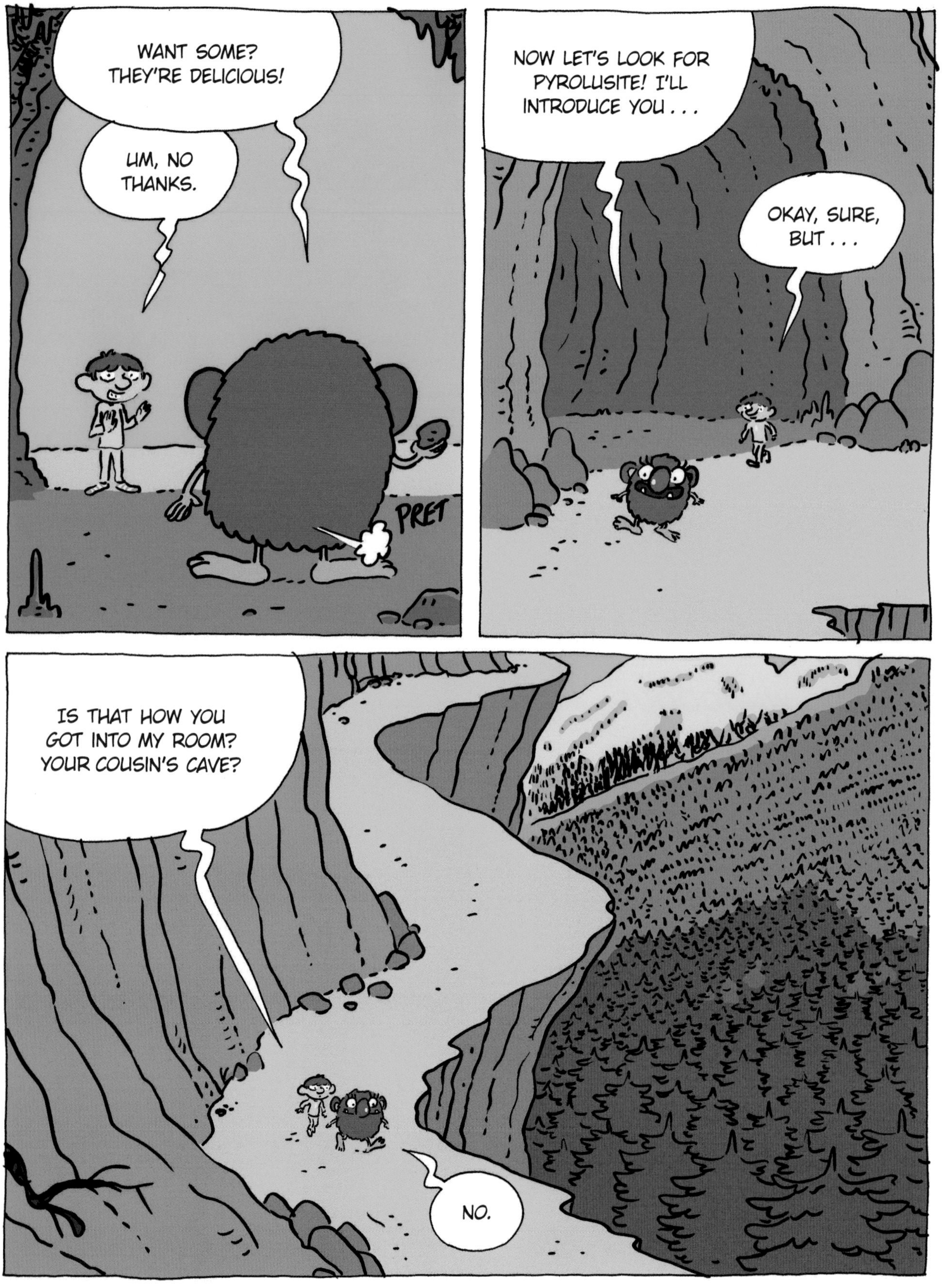
WANT SOME? THEY'RE DELICIOUS!
UM, NO THANKS.
PRET
NOW LET'S LOOK FOR PYROLUSITE! I'LL INTRODUCE YOU . . .
OKAY, SURE, BUT . . .
IS THAT HOW YOU GOT INTO MY ROOM? YOUR COUSIN'S CAVE?
NO.

THE GNOMES WERE BULLYING ME, SO I HID INSIDE A HOLLOW TREE TRUNK.

THE WHA . . . ?

HEY!

SOMETHING JUST STUNG ME!

!?!?

A TINY ARROW?

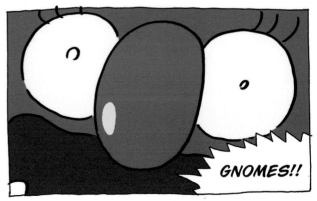

GNOMES!!

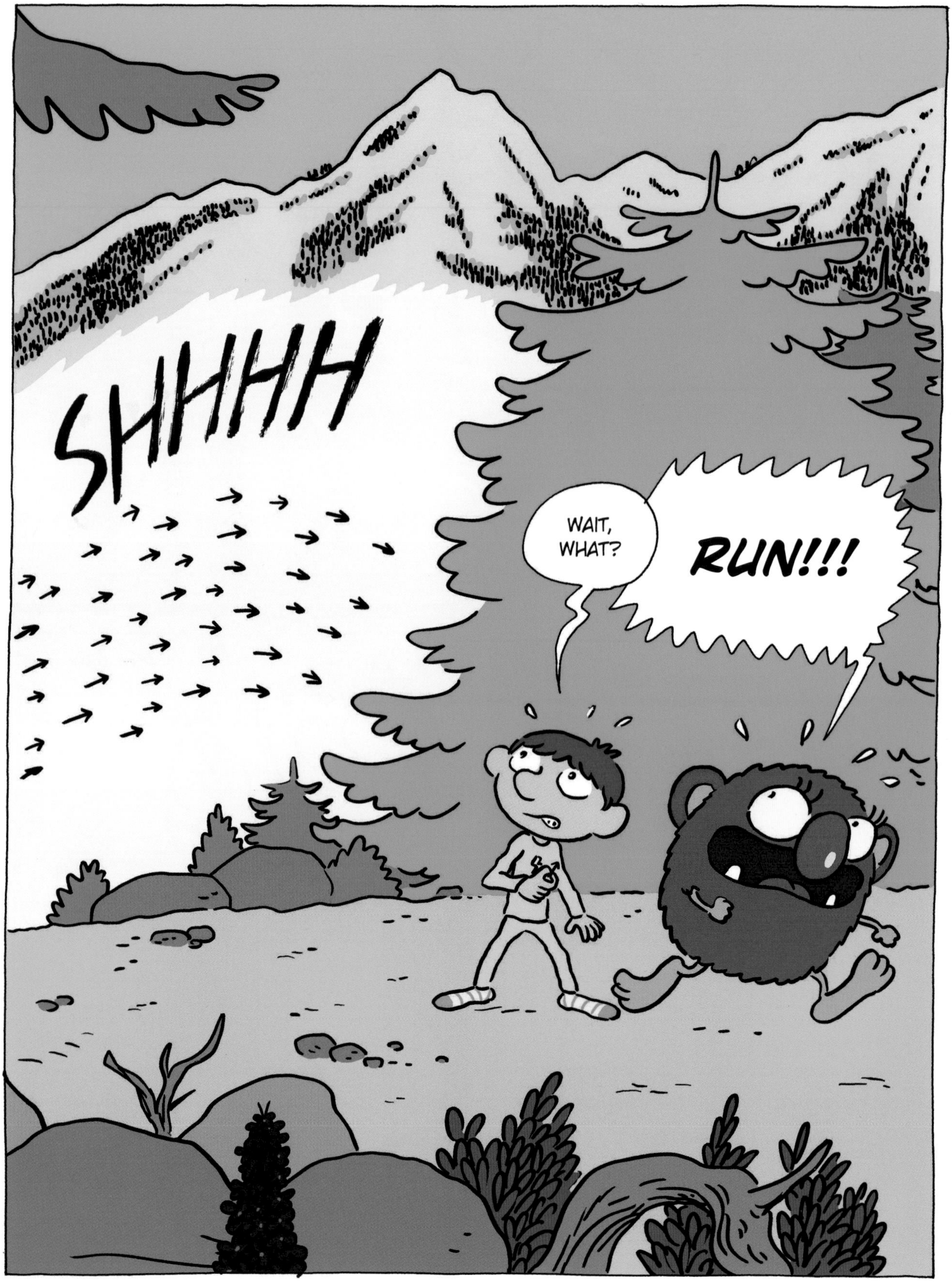
SHHHH
WAIT, WHAT?
RUN!!!

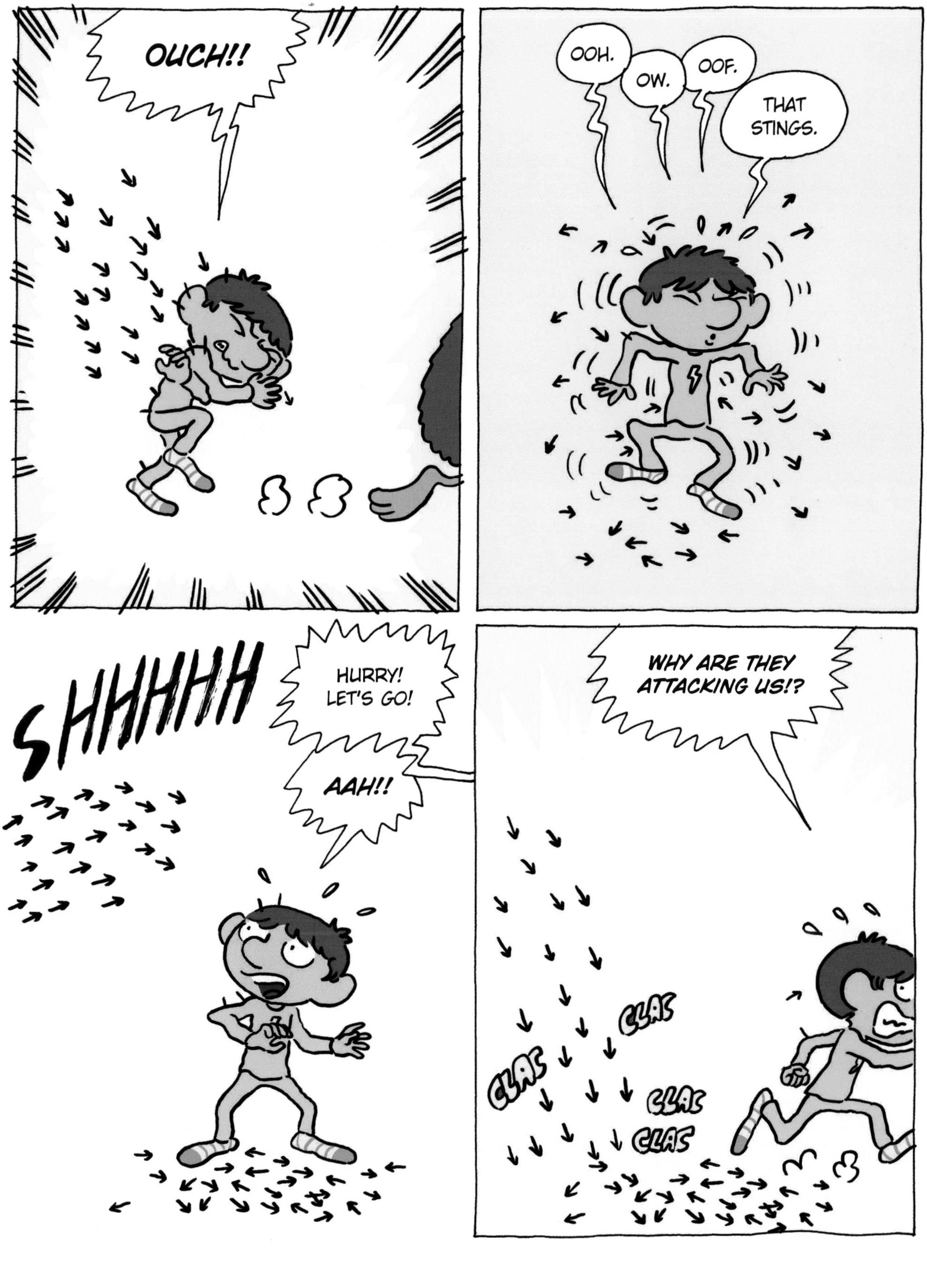
OUCH!!
OOH.
OW.
OOF.
THAT STINGS.
SHHHHHH
HURRY! LET'S GO!
AAH!!
WHY ARE THEY ATTACKING US!?
CLAC
CLAC
CLAC
CLAC

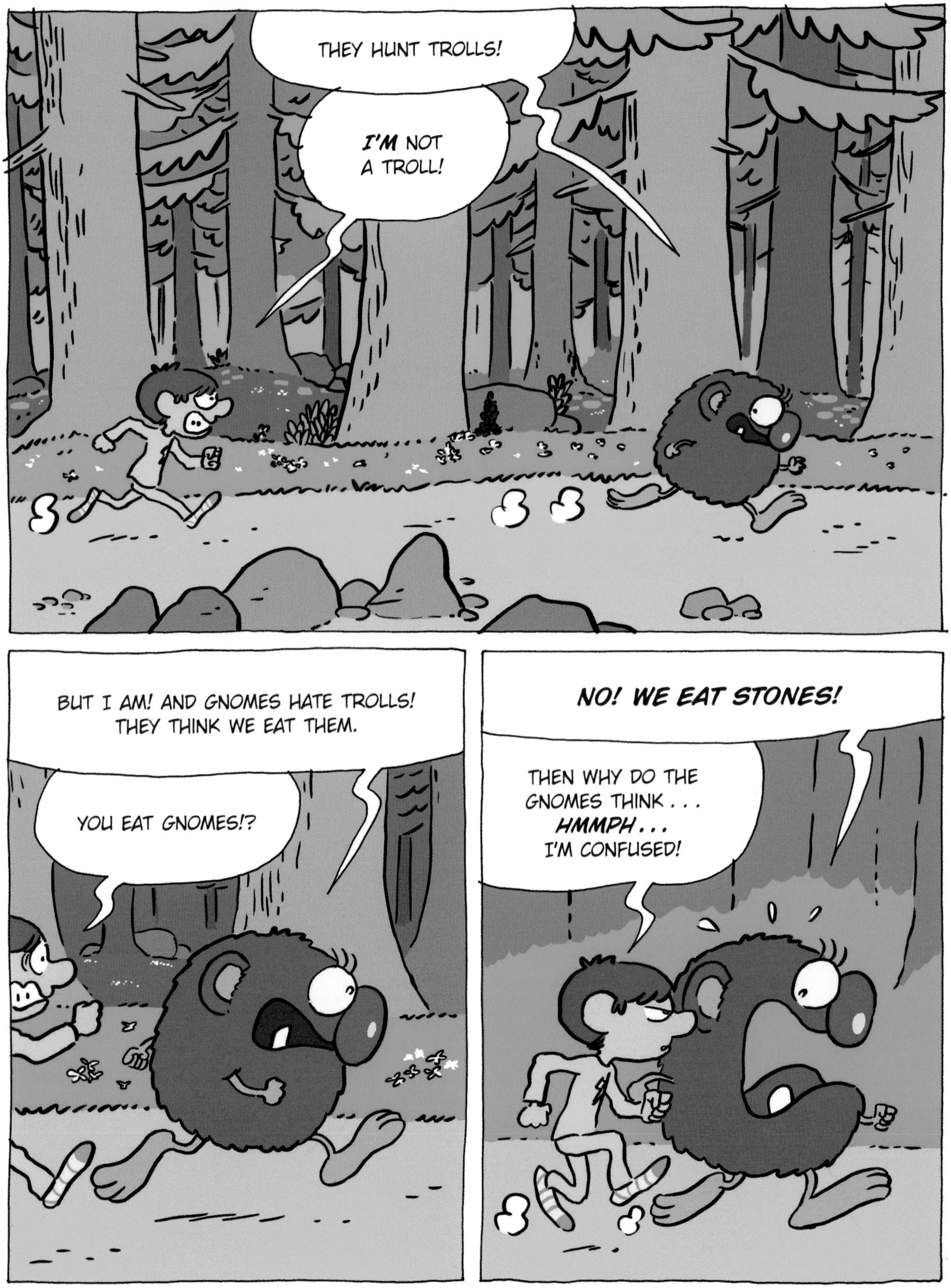
THEY HUNT TROLLS!
I'M NOT A TROLL!
BUT I AM! AND GNOMES HATE TROLLS! THEY THINK WE EAT THEM.
YOU EAT GNOMES!?
NO! WE EAT STONES!
THEN WHY DO THE GNOMES THINK . . . HMMPH . . . I'M CONFUSED!

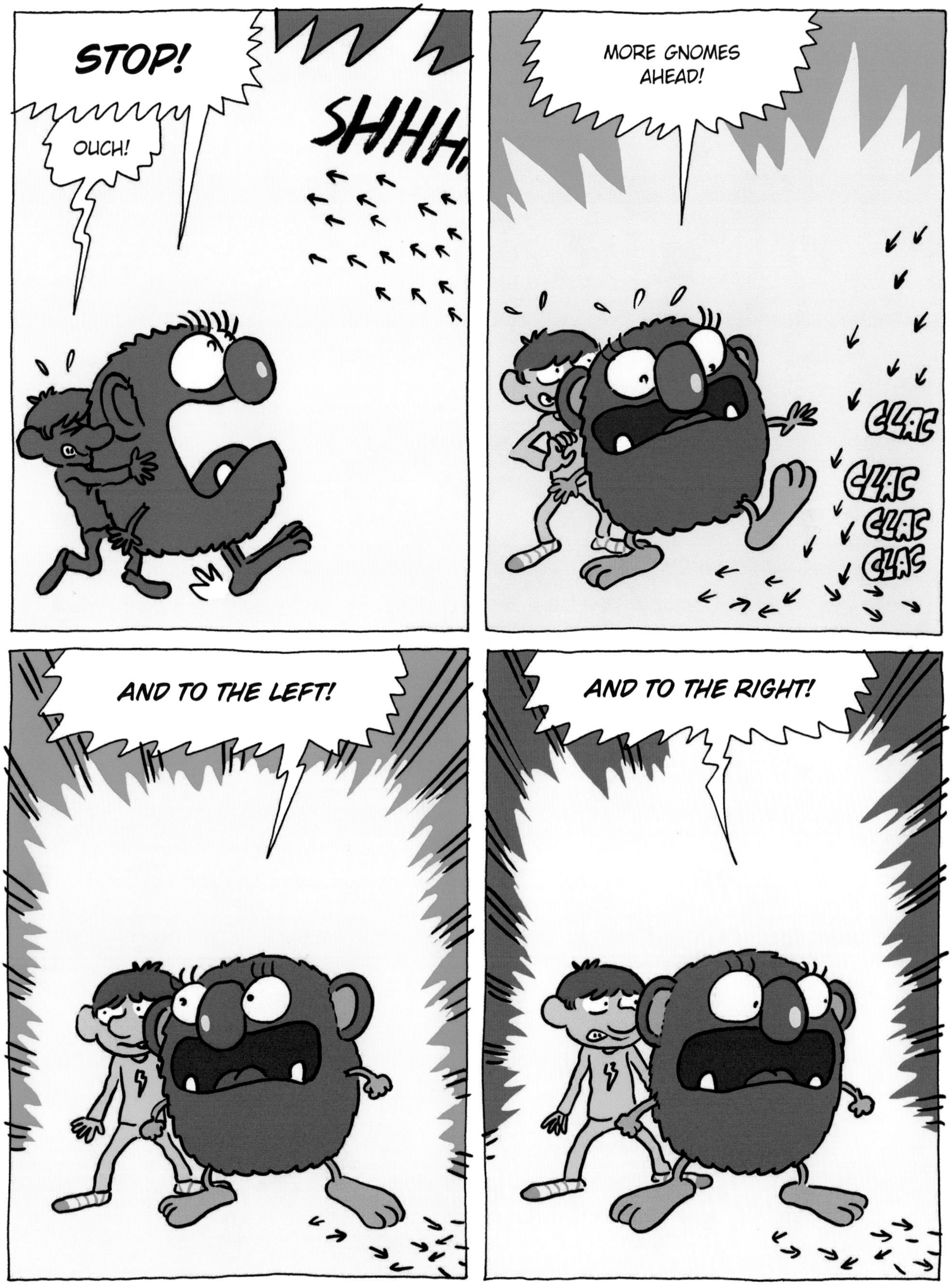
STOP!
OUCH!
SHHH
MORE GNOMES AHEAD!
CLAC
CLAC
CLAC
CLAC
AND TO THE LEFT!
AND TO THE RIGHT!

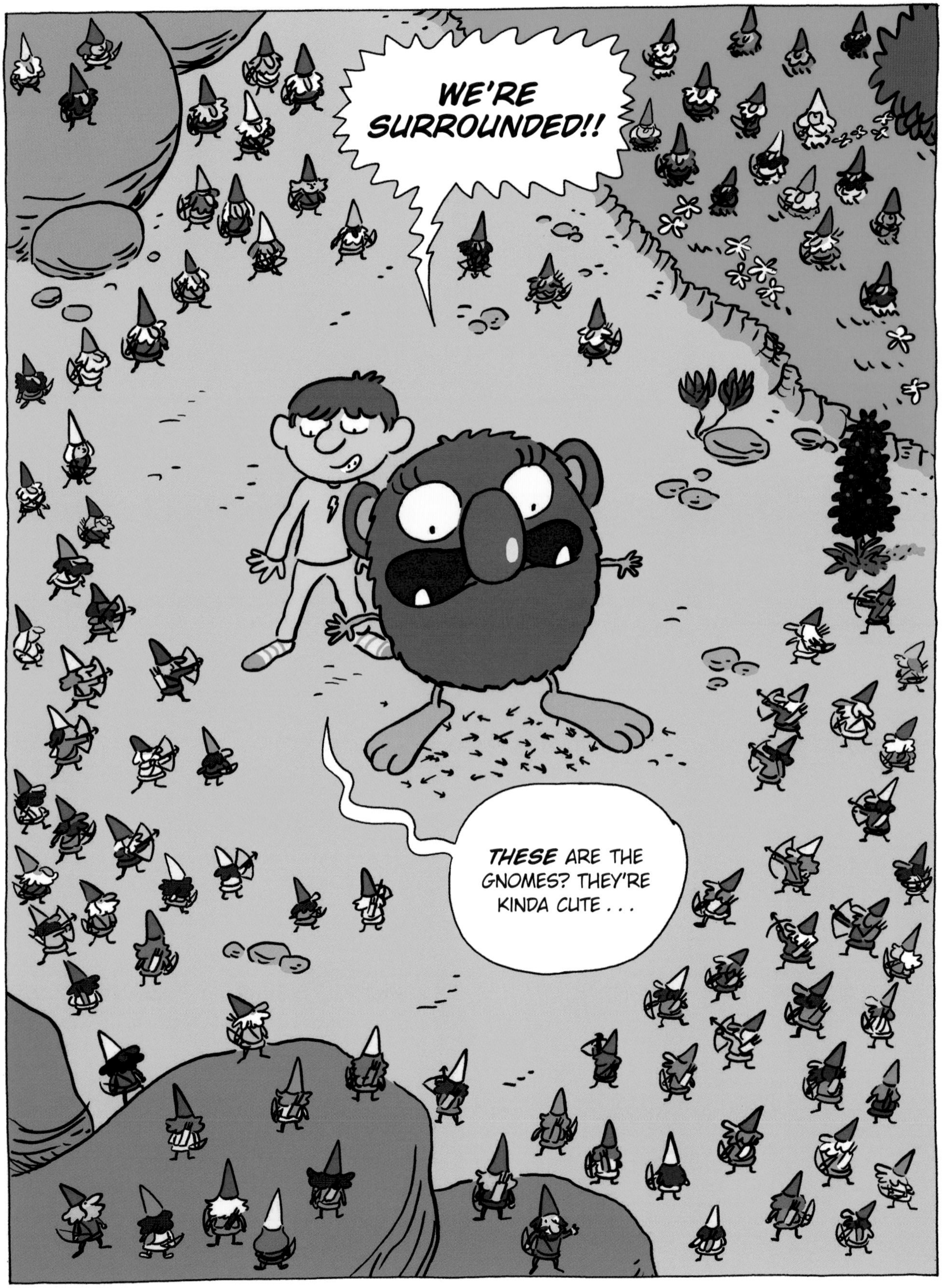
WE'RE SURROUNDED!!
THESE ARE THE GNOMES? THEY'RE KINDA CUTE . . .

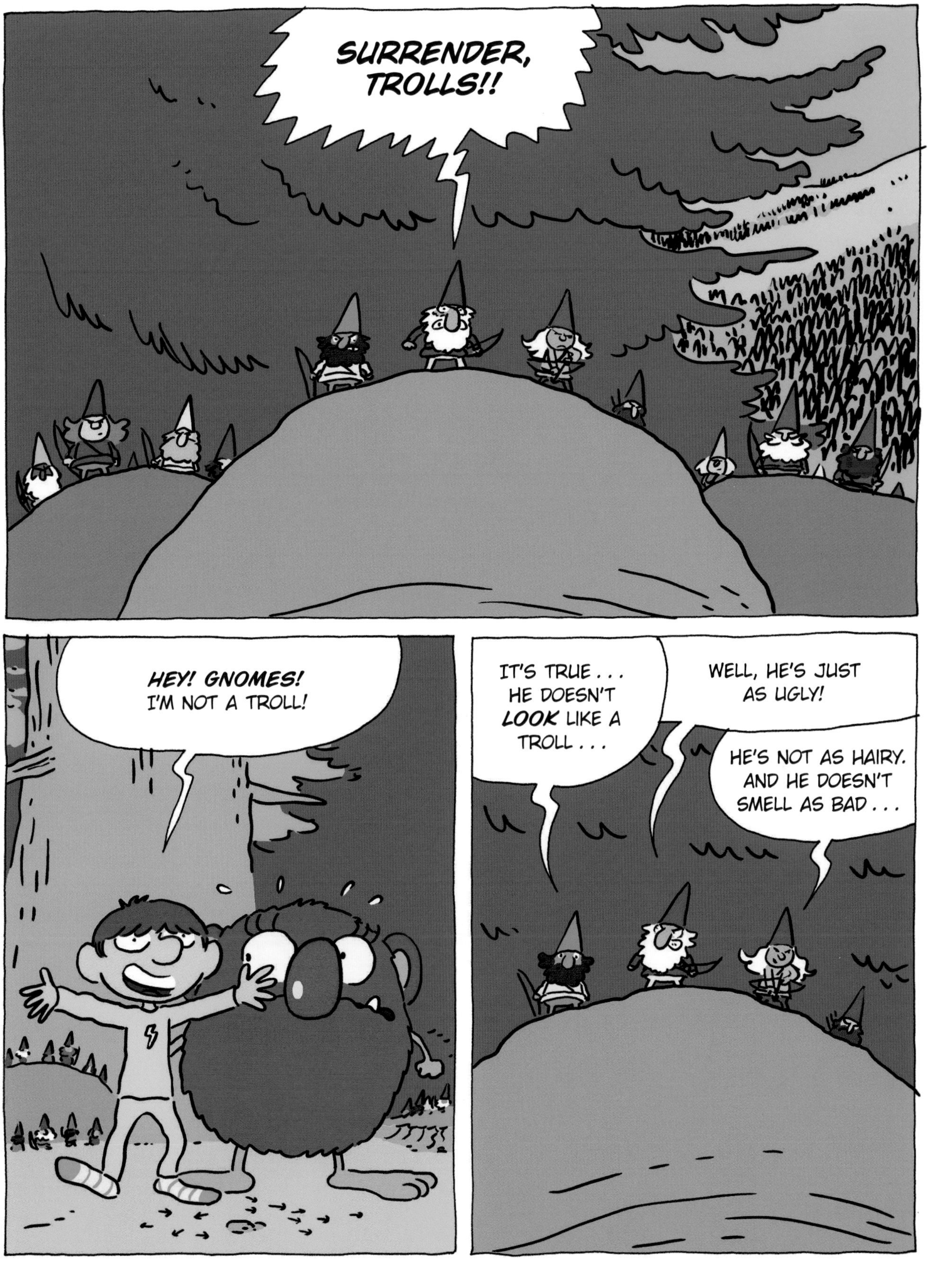
SURRENDER, TROLLS!!
HEY! GNOMES! I'M NOT A TROLL!
IT'S TRUE . . . HE DOESN'T LOOK LIKE A TROLL . . .
WELL, HE'S JUST AS UGLY!
HE'S NOT AS HAIRY. AND HE DOESN'T SMELL AS BAD . . .

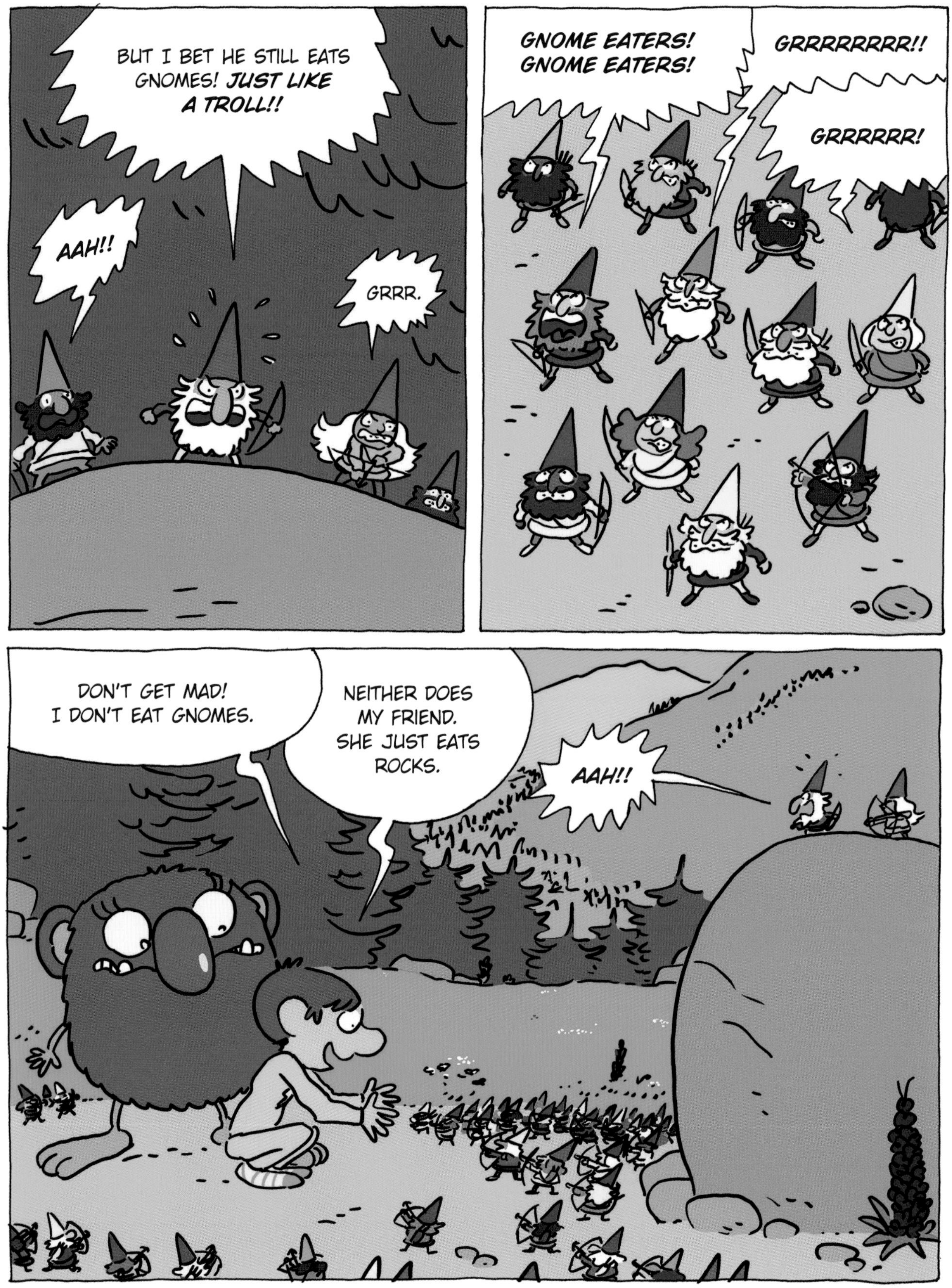
BUT I BET HE STILL EATS GNOMES! **JUST LIKE A TROLL!!**
AAH!!
GRRR.
GNOME EATERS! GNOME EATERS!
GRRRRRRRR!!
GRRRRRR!
DON'T GET MAD! I DON'T EAT GNOMES.
NEITHER DOES MY FRIEND. SHE JUST EATS ROCKS.
AAH!!

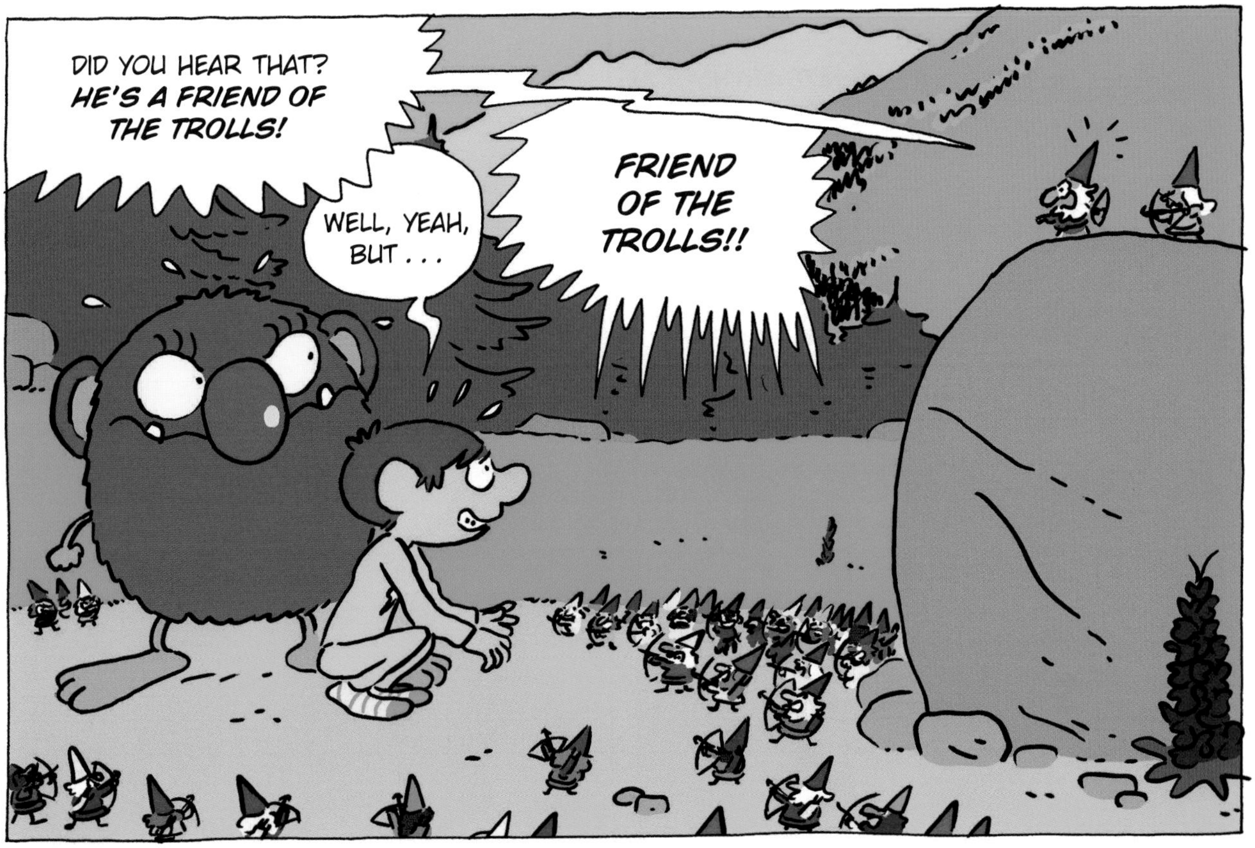
DID YOU HEAR THAT? HE'S A FRIEND OF THE TROLLS!
WELL, YEAH, BUT . . .
FRIEND OF THE TROLLS!!

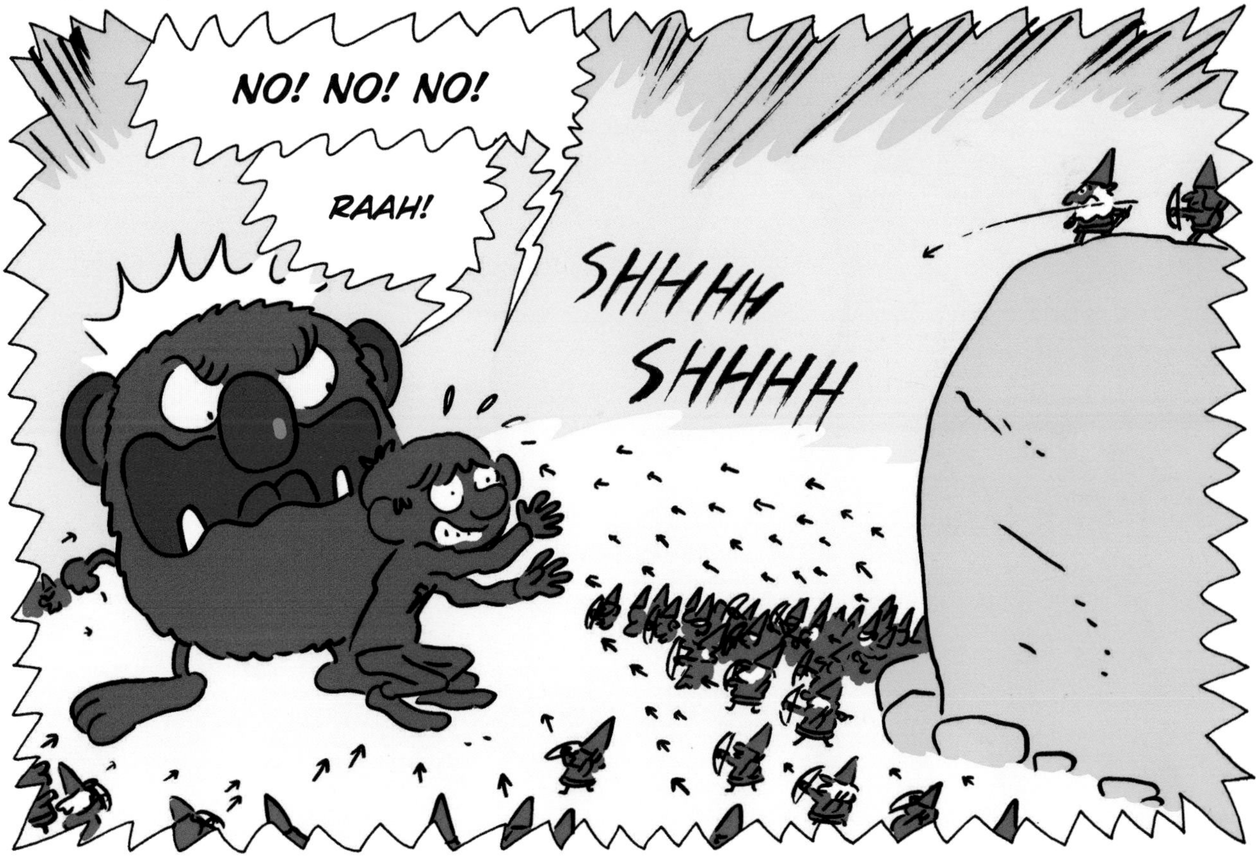
NO! NO! NO!
RAAH!
SHHHH
SHHHH

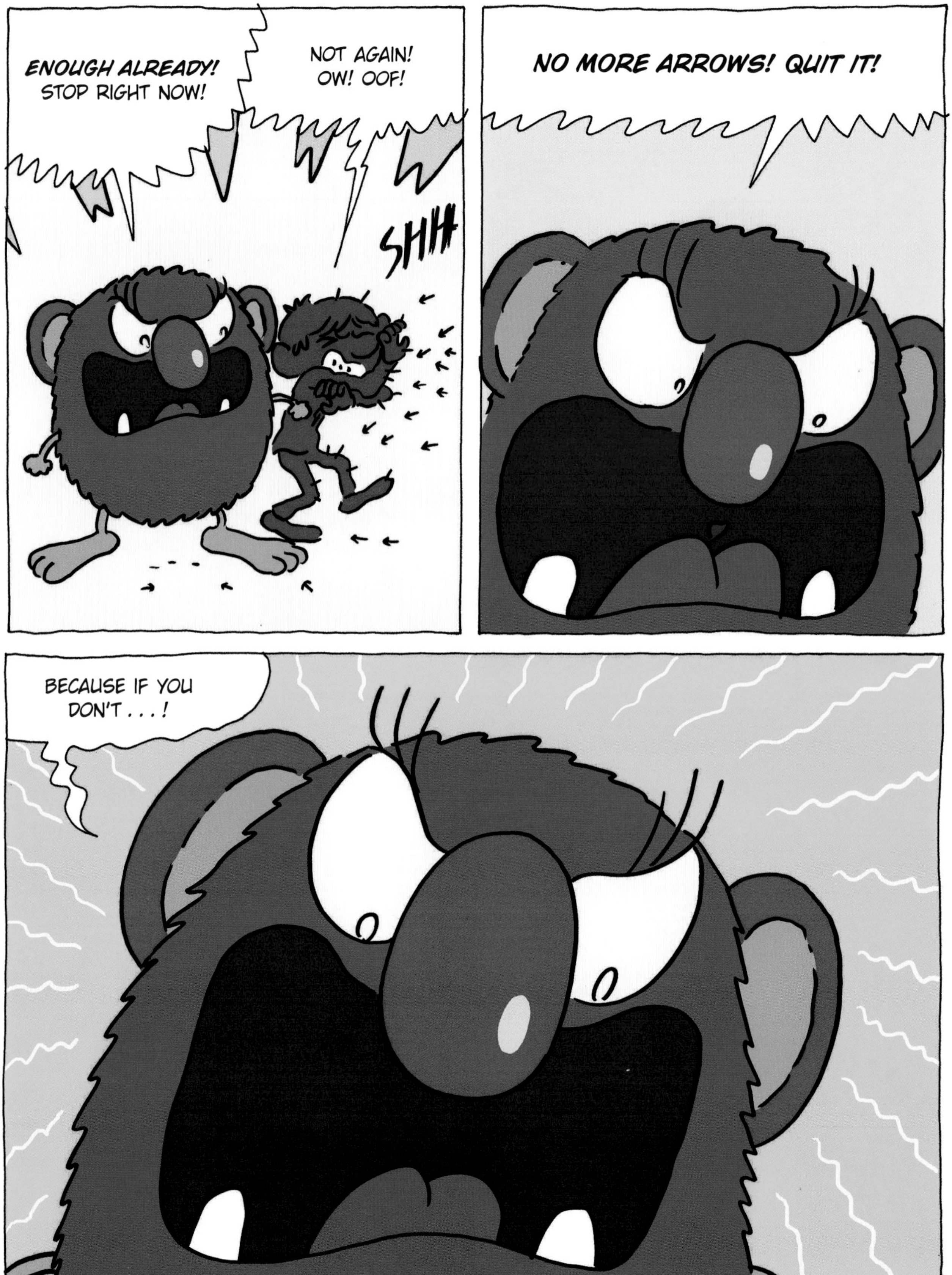
ENOUGH ALREADY! STOP RIGHT NOW!
NOT AGAIN! OW! OOF!
SHH
NO MORE ARROWS! QUIT IT!
BECAUSE IF YOU DON'T . . . !

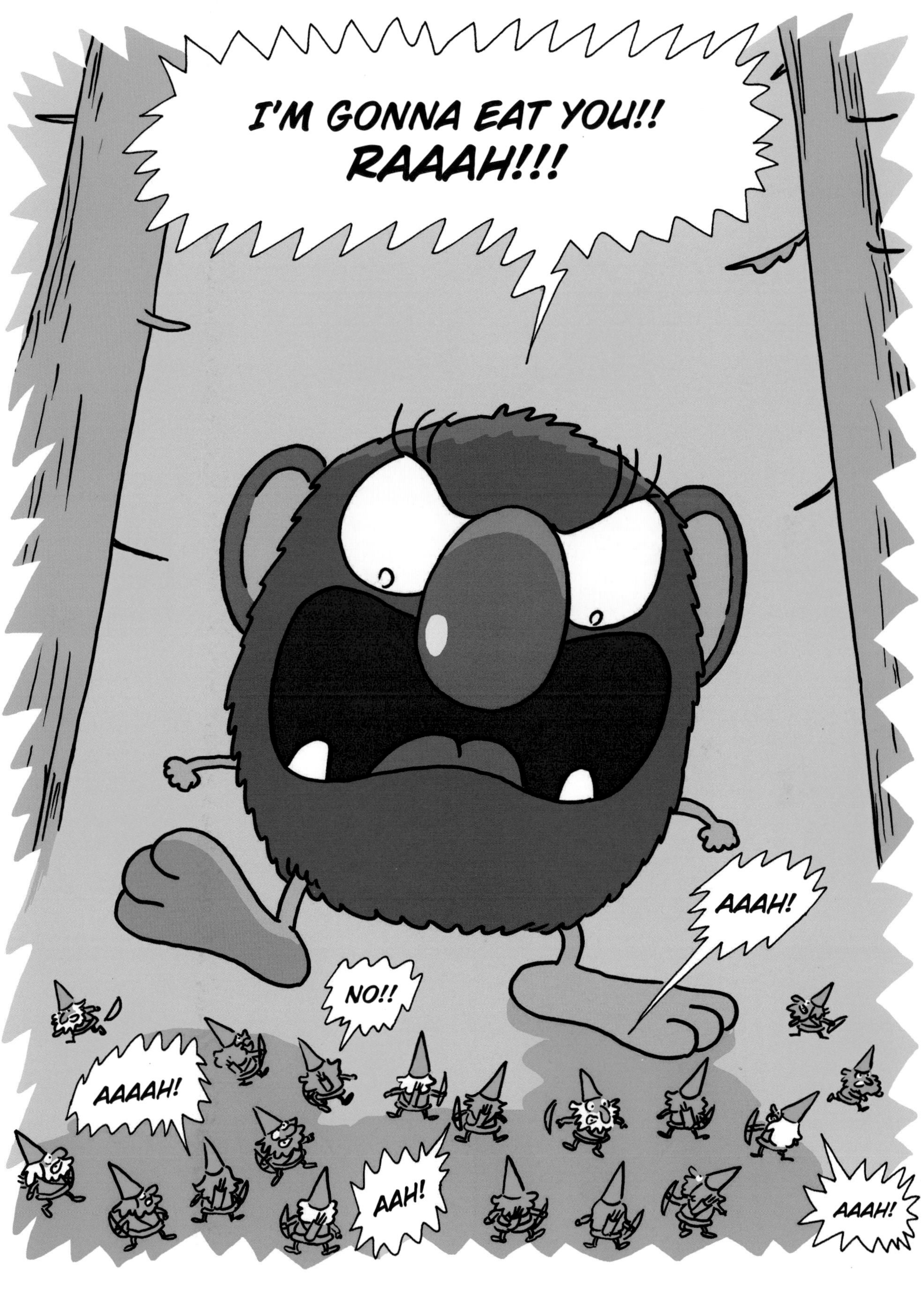
I'M GONNA EAT YOU!!
RAAAH!!!
NO!!
AAAH!
AAAAH!
AAH!
AAAH!

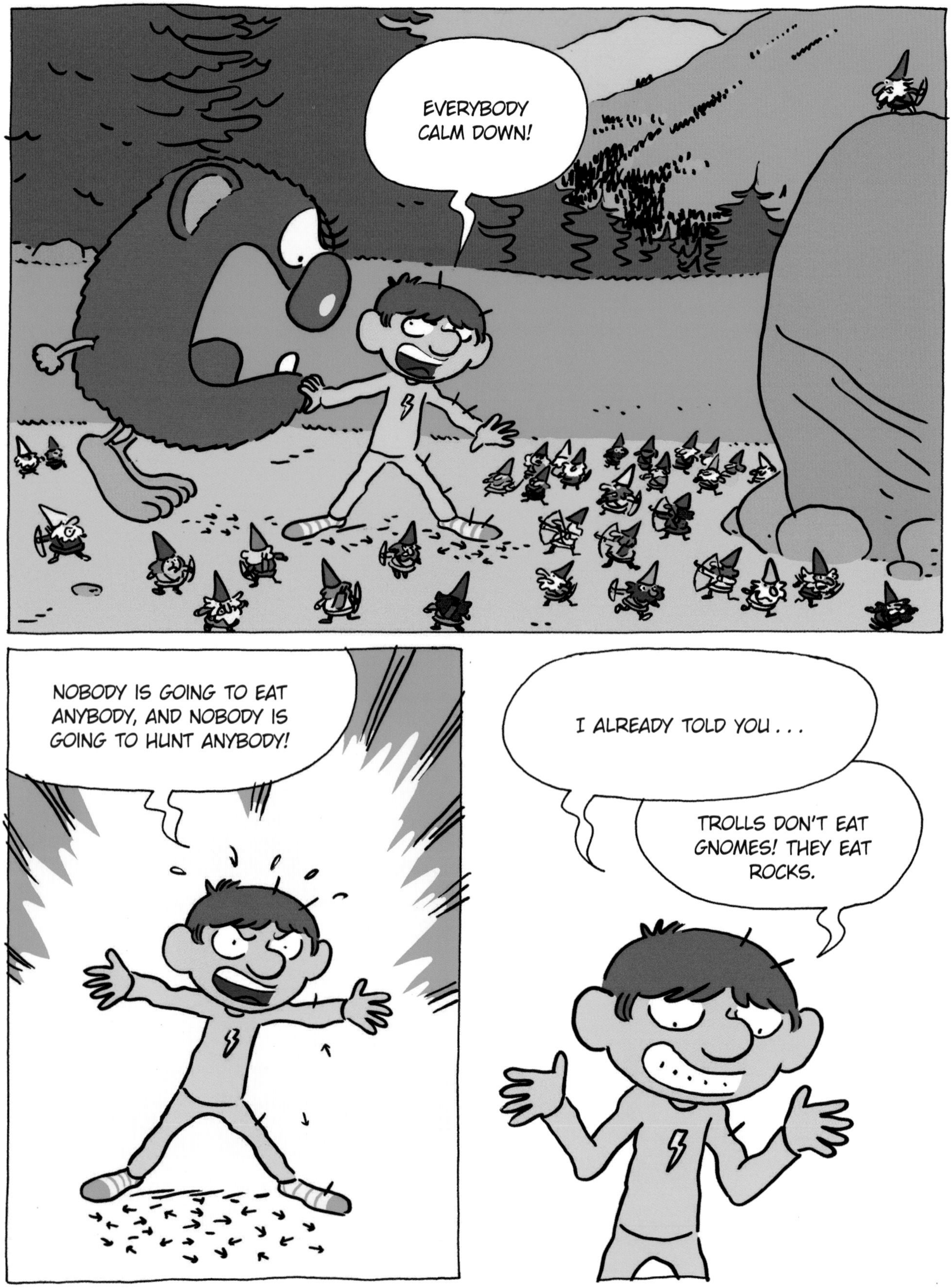
EVERYBODY CALM DOWN!
NOBODY IS GOING TO EAT ANYBODY, AND NOBODY IS GOING TO HUNT ANYBODY!
I ALREADY TOLD YOU . . .
TROLLS DON'T EAT GNOMES! THEY EAT ROCKS.

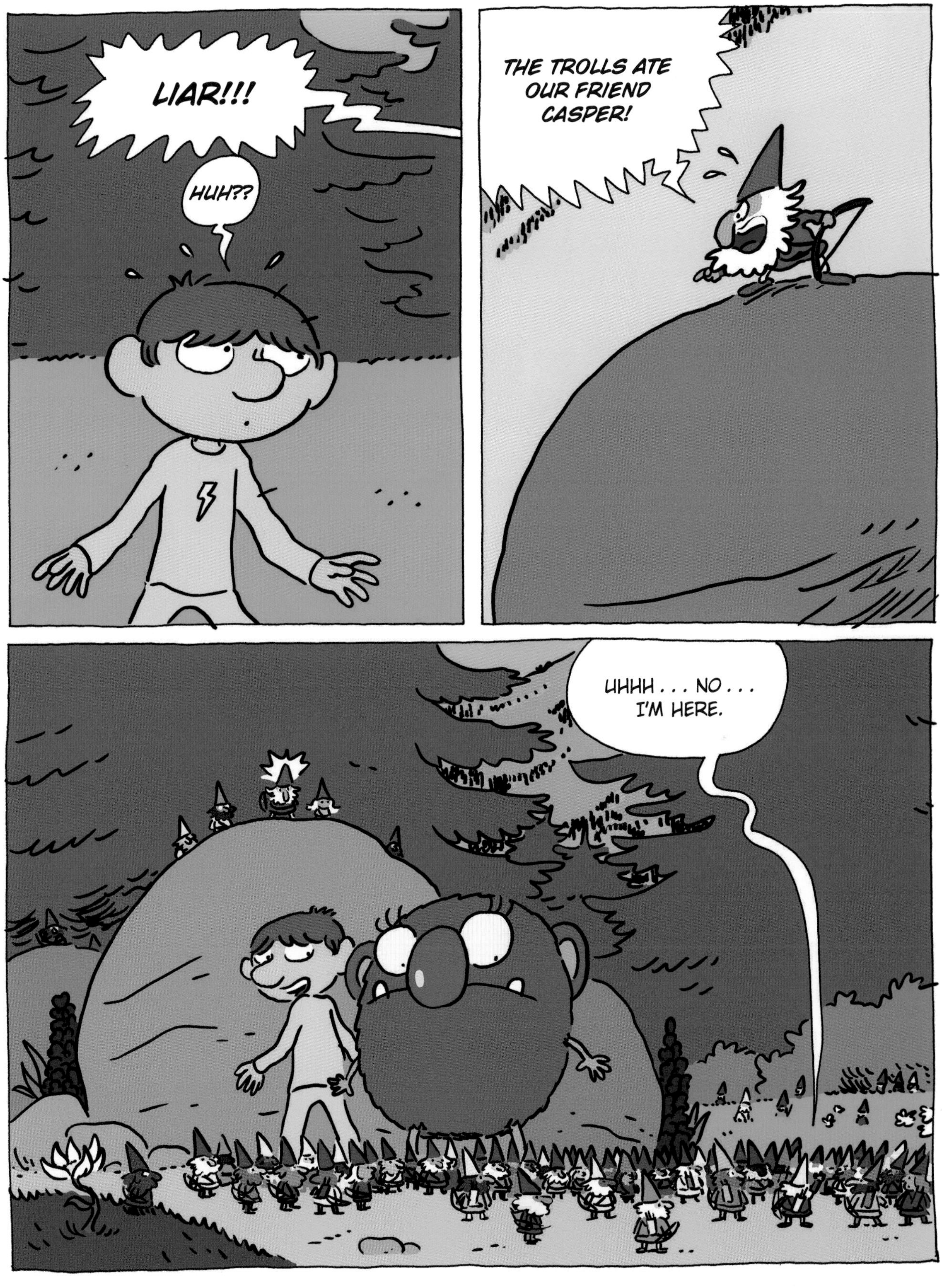
LIAR!!!
HUH??
THE TROLLS ATE OUR FRIEND CASPER!
UHHH . . . NO . . . I'M HERE.

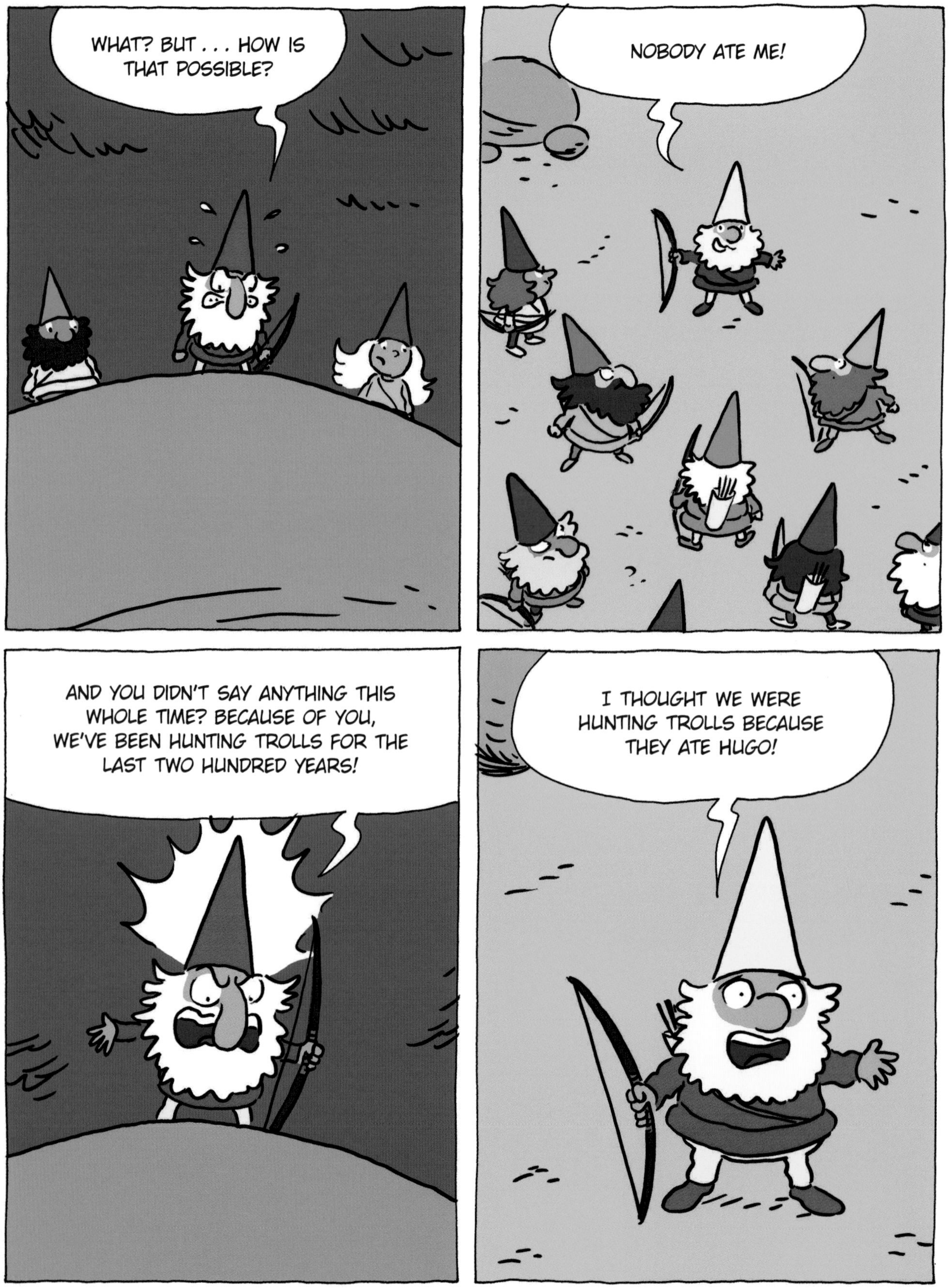
WHAT? BUT . . . HOW IS THAT POSSIBLE?
NOBODY ATE ME!
AND YOU DIDN'T SAY ANYTHING THIS WHOLE TIME? BECAUSE OF YOU, WE'VE BEEN HUNTING TROLLS FOR THE LAST TWO HUNDRED YEARS!
I THOUGHT WE WERE HUNTING TROLLS BECAUSE THEY ATE HUGO!

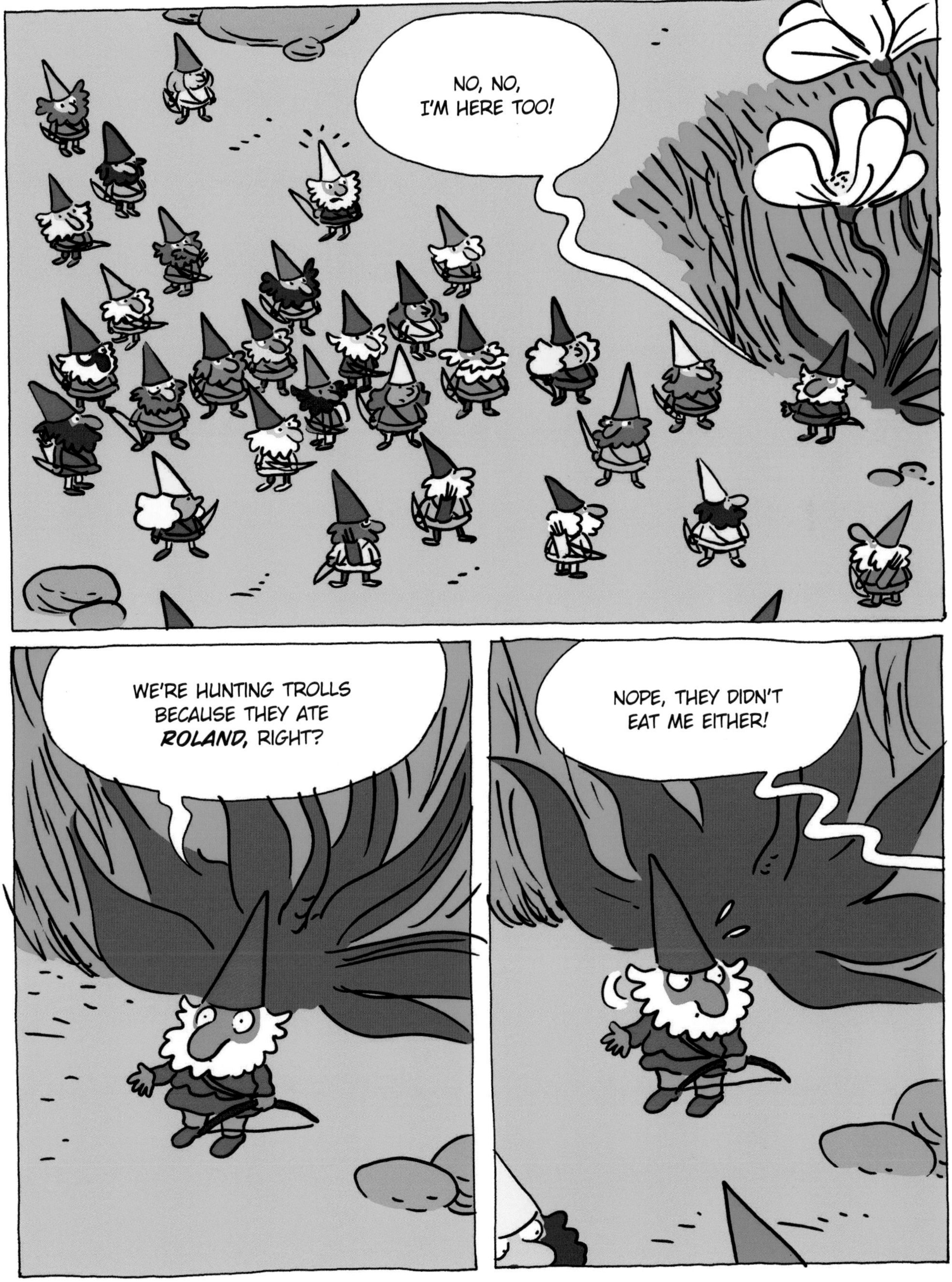
NO, NO, I'M HERE TOO!
WE'RE HUNTING TROLLS BECAUSE THEY ATE **ROLAND,** RIGHT?
NOPE, THEY DIDN'T EAT ME EITHER!

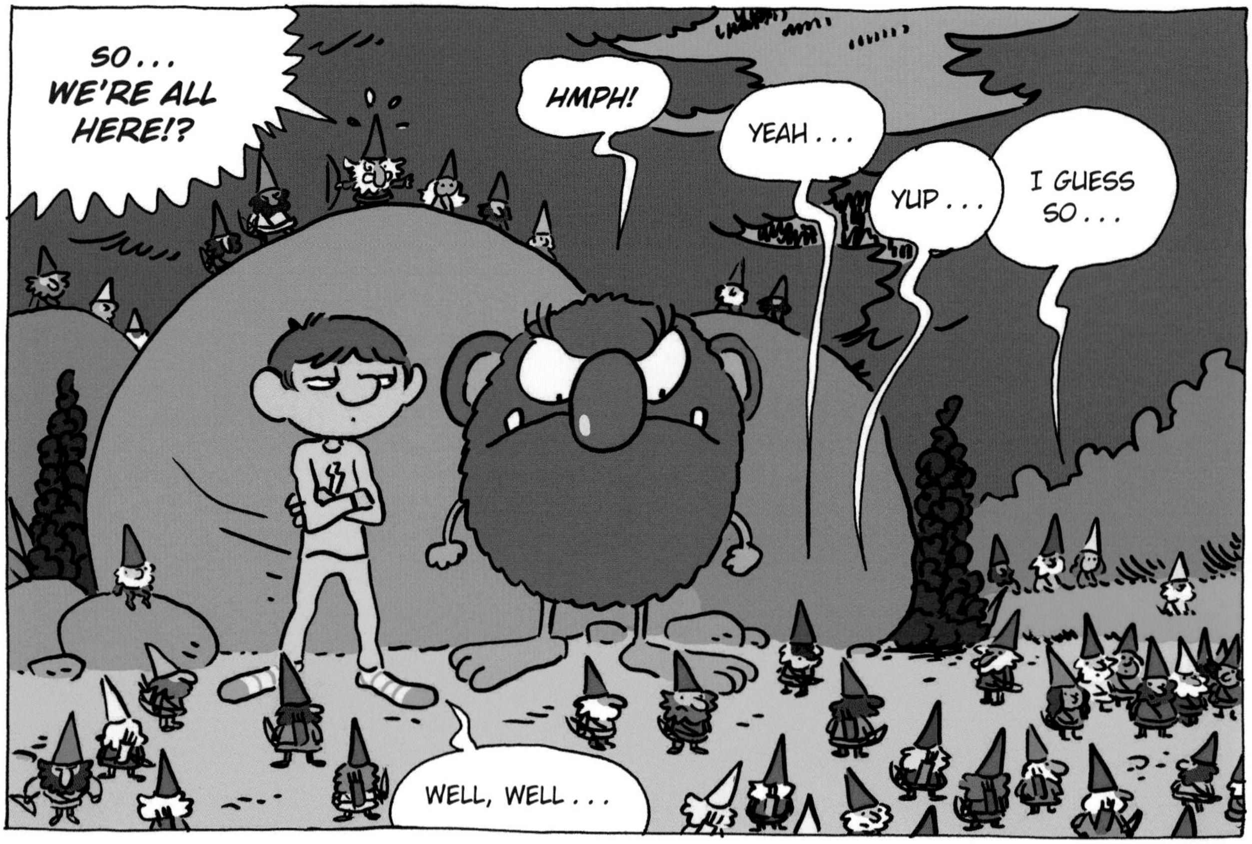
SO . . .
WE'RE ALL HERE!?
HMPH!
YEAH . . .
YUP . . .
I GUESS SO . . .
WELL, WELL . . .

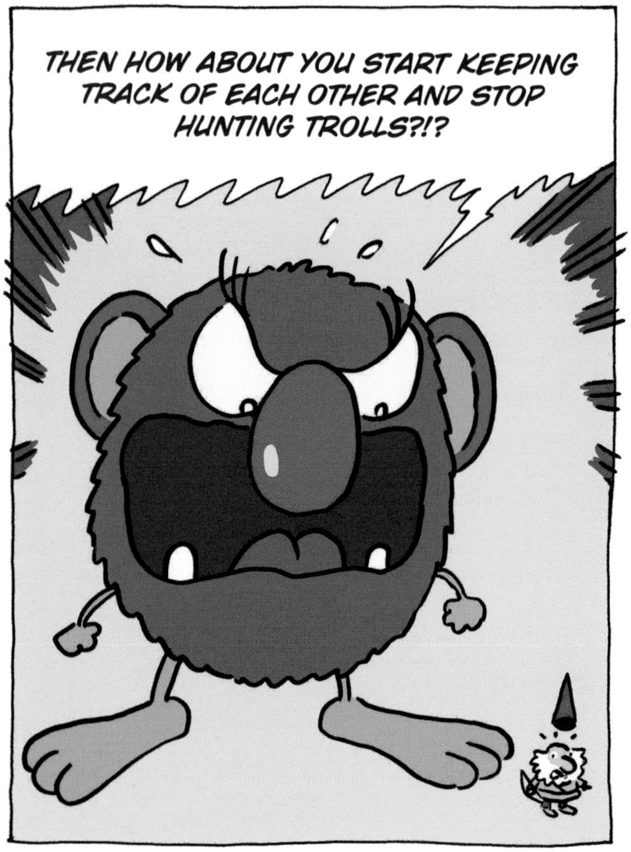
THEN HOW ABOUT YOU START KEEPING TRACK OF EACH OTHER AND STOP HUNTING TROLLS?!?

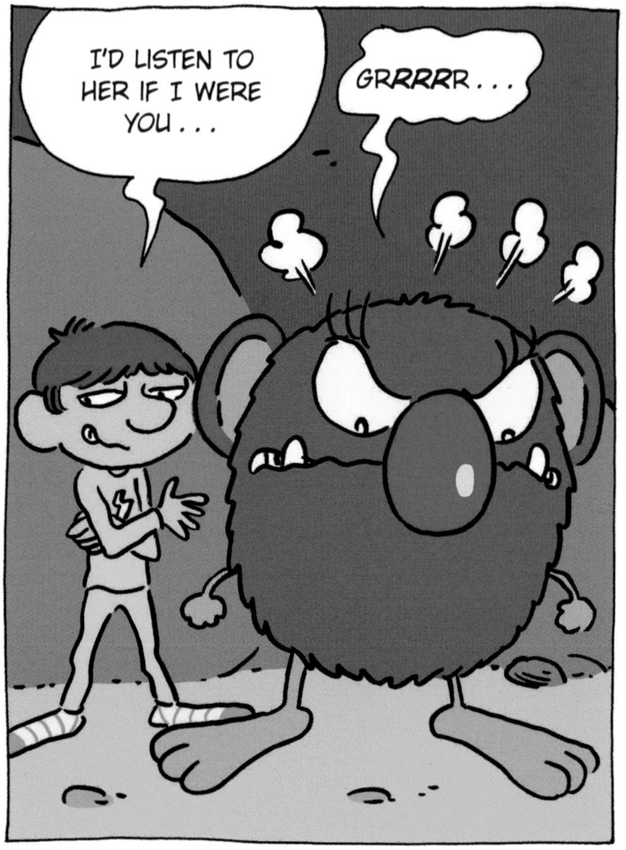
I'D LISTEN TO HER IF I WERE YOU . . .
GRRRRR . . .

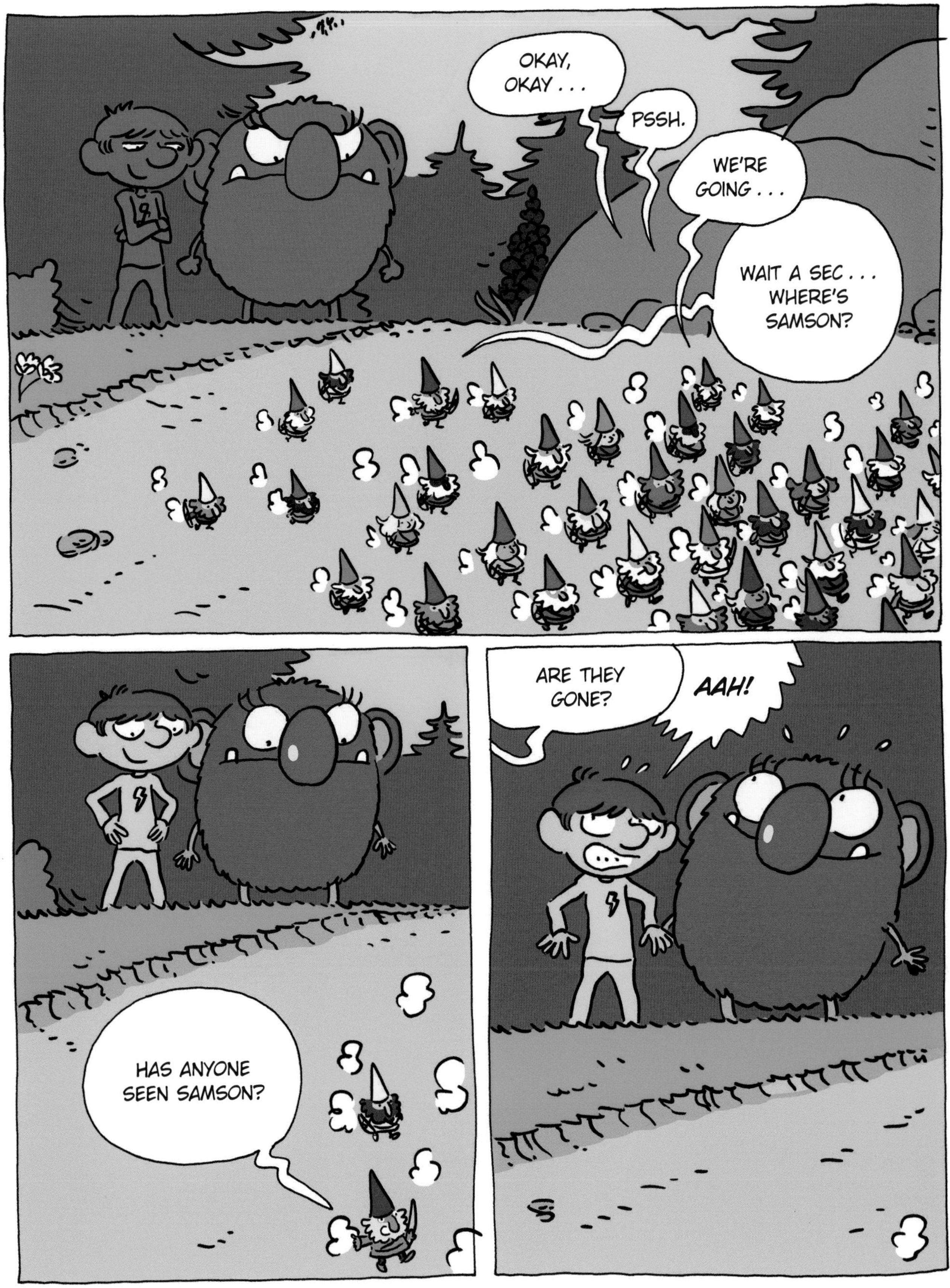
OKAY, OKAY . . .
PSSH.
WE'RE GOING . . .
WAIT A SEC . . . WHERE'S SAMSON?
HAS ANYONE SEEN SAMSON?
ARE THEY GONE?
AAH!

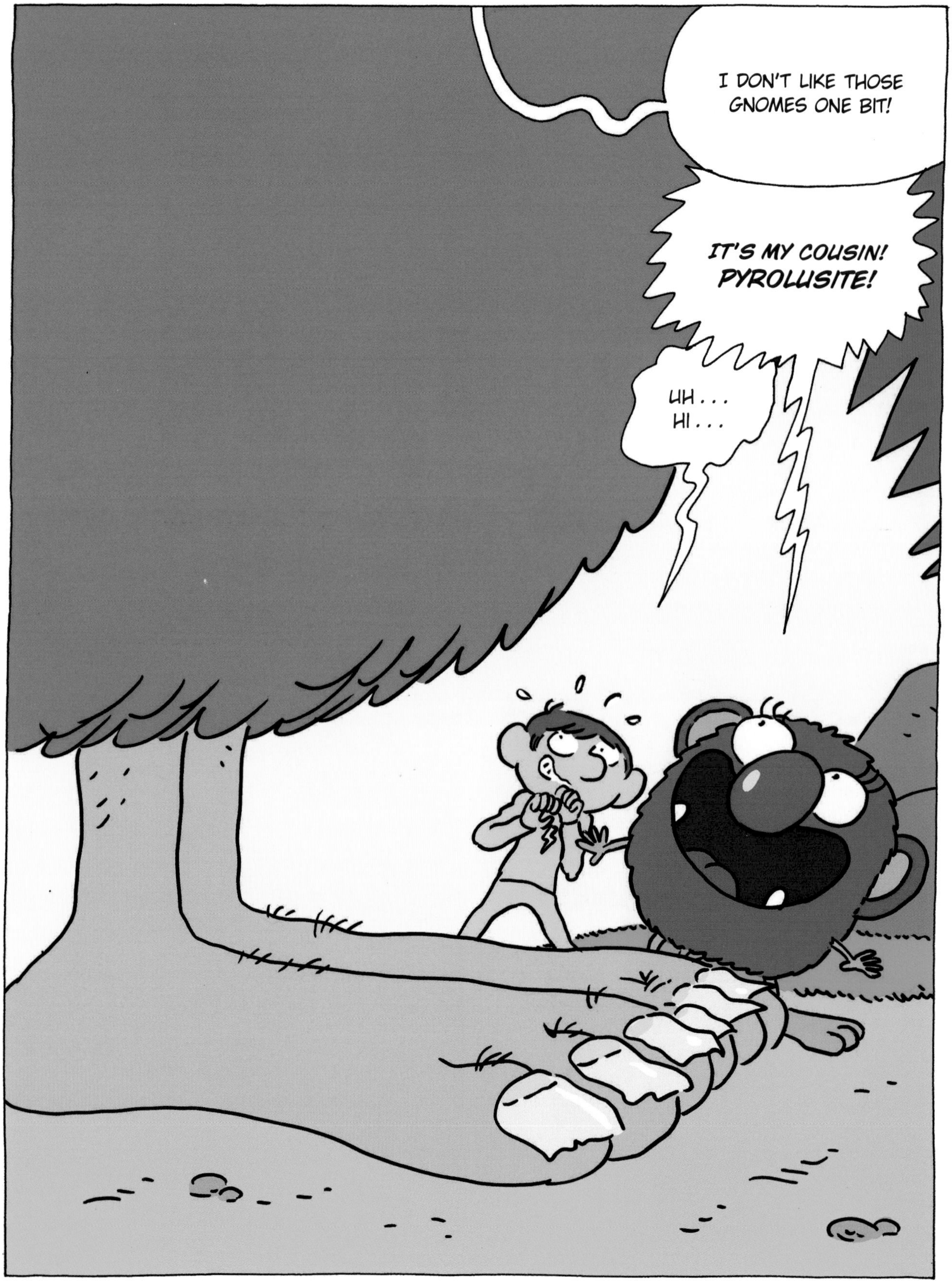
I DON'T LIKE THOSE GNOMES ONE BIT!
IT'S MY COUSIN! PYROLUSITE!
UH . . . HI . . .

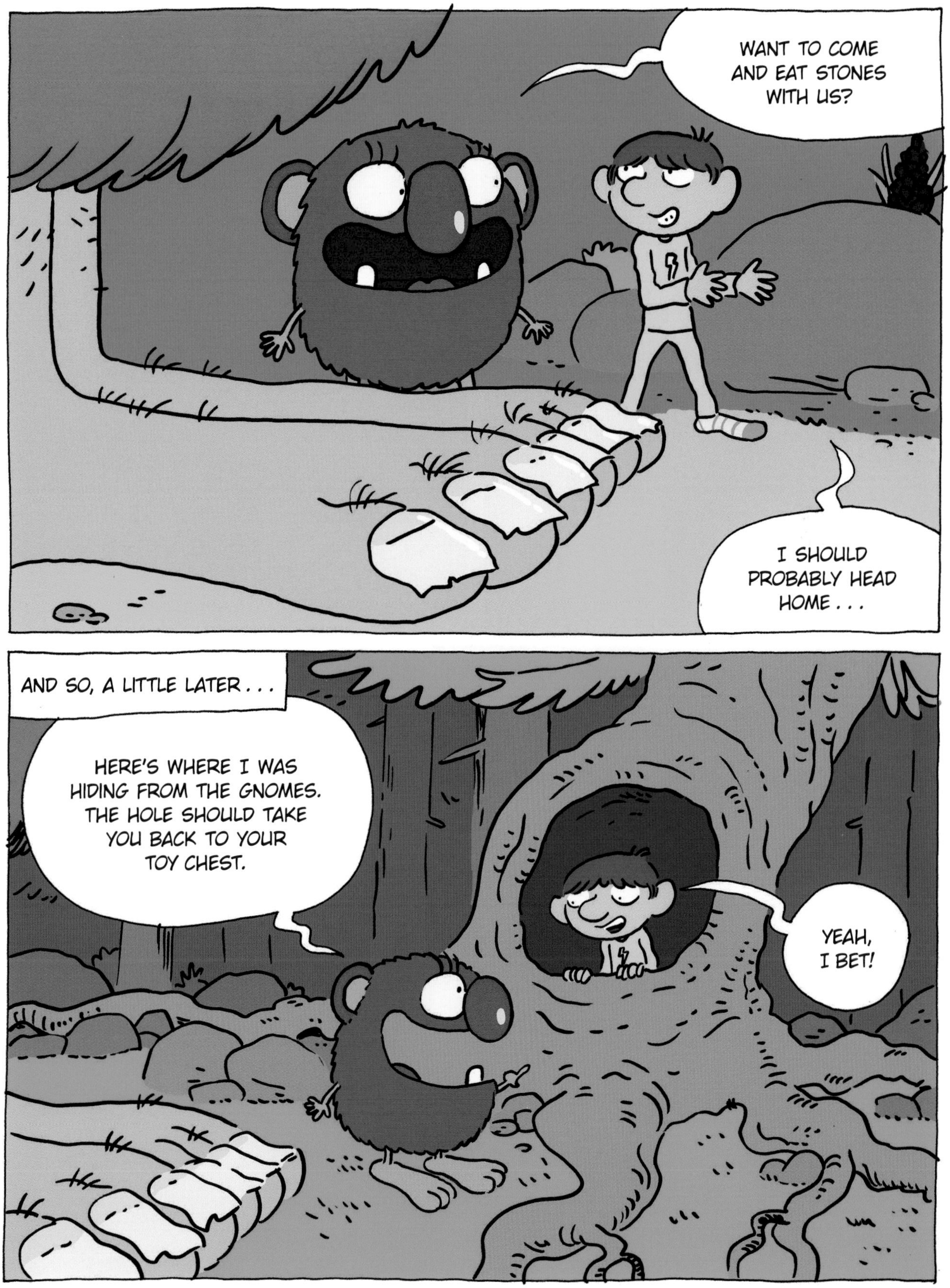
WANT TO COME AND EAT STONES WITH US?
I SHOULD PROBABLY HEAD HOME . . .
AND SO, A LITTLE LATER . . .
HERE'S WHERE I WAS HIDING FROM THE GNOMES. THE HOLE SHOULD TAKE YOU BACK TO YOUR TOY CHEST.
YEAH, I BET!

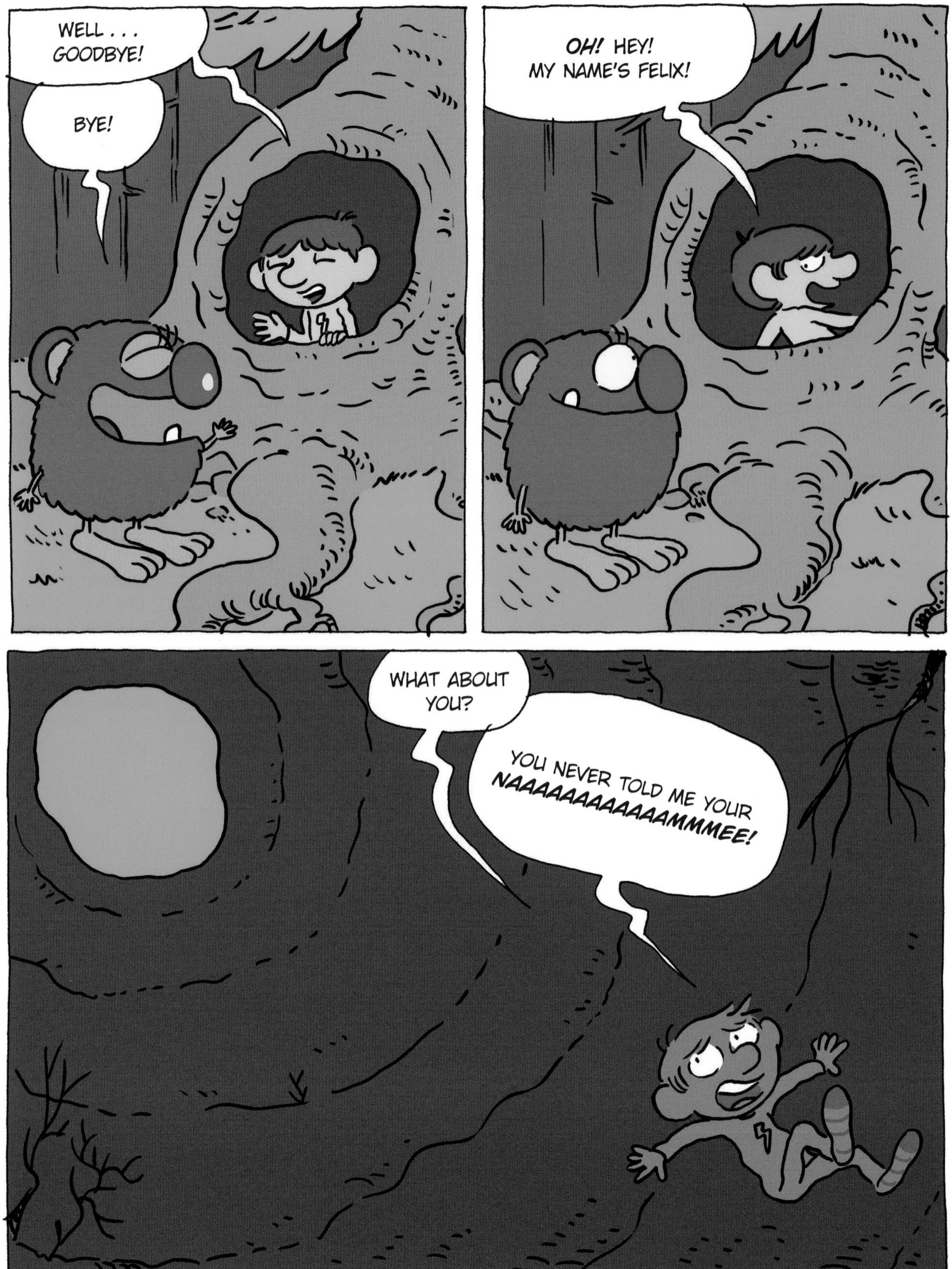
WELL . . . GOODBYE!
BYE!
OH! HEY! MY NAME'S FELIX!
WHAT ABOUT YOU?
YOU NEVER TOLD ME YOUR NAAAAAAAAAAAAMMMEE!

IT'S TRUE. THE LITTLE TROLL HASN'T GIVEN FELIX HER NAME . . .

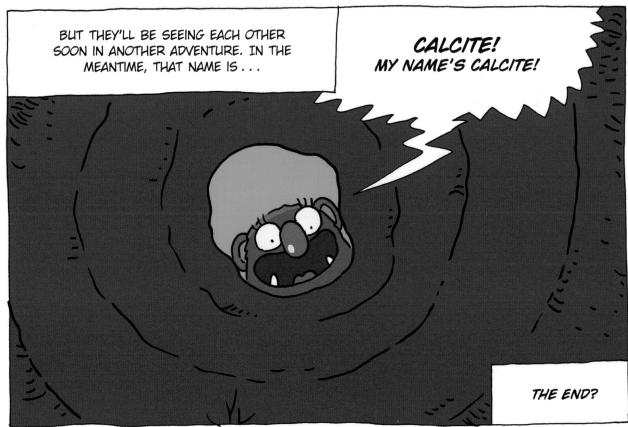

BUT THEY'LL BE SEEING EACH OTHER SOON IN ANOTHER ADVENTURE. IN THE MEANTIME, THAT NAME IS . . .

CALCITE!
MY NAME'S CALCITE!

THE END?

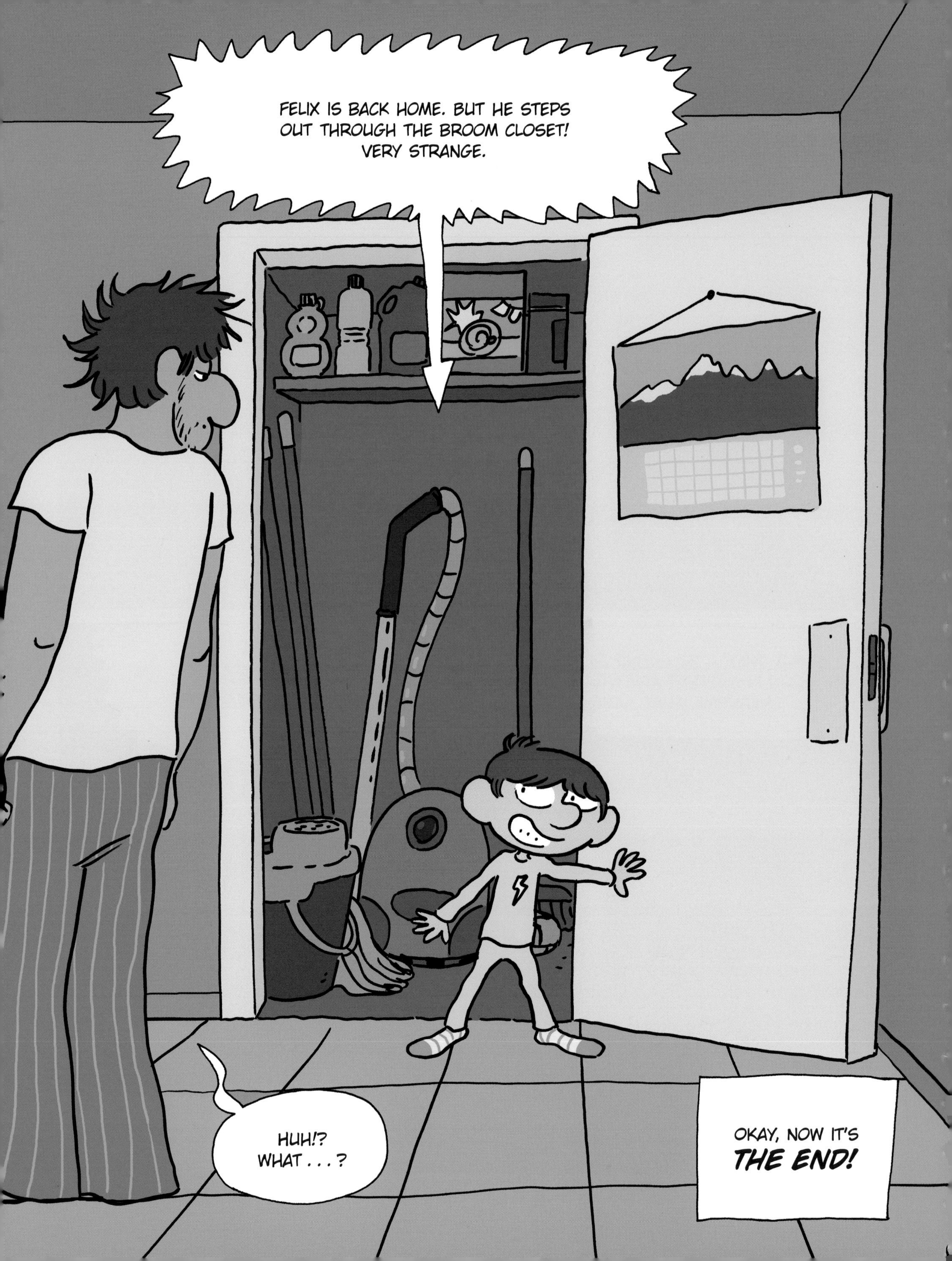
FELIX IS BACK HOME. BUT HE STEPS OUT THROUGH THE BROOM CLOSET! VERY STRANGE.
HUH!? WHAT . . . ?
OKAY, NOW IT'S THE END!

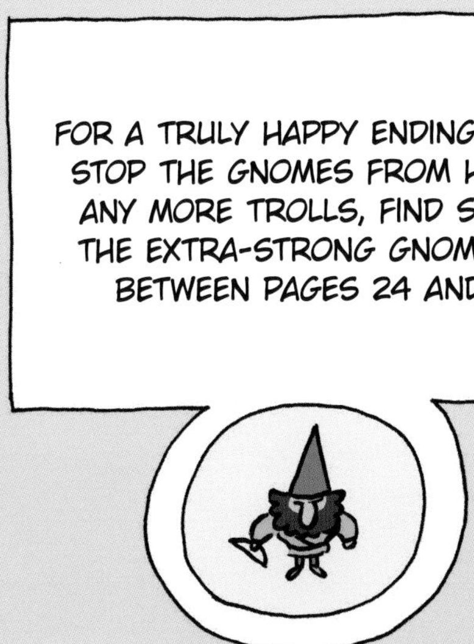
FOR A TRULY HAPPY ENDING, AND TO STOP THE GNOMES FROM HUNTING ANY MORE TROLLS, FIND SAMSON THE EXTRA-STRONG GNOME. HE'S BETWEEN PAGES 24 AND 35.

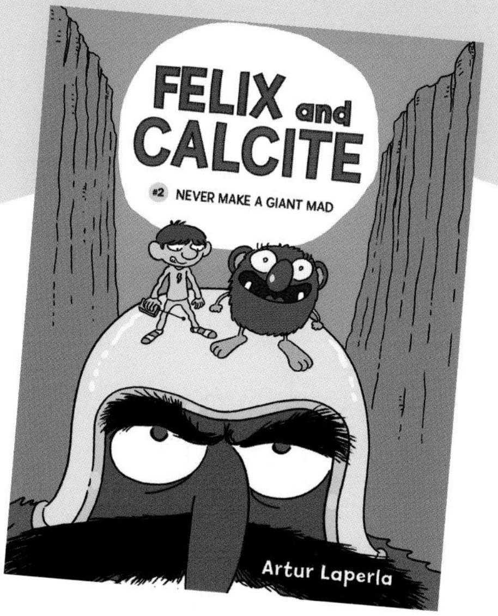
FELIX and CALCITE
#2 NEVER MAKE A GIANT MAD
Artur Laperla

AND LOOK OUT FOR
THE NEXT ADVENTURE OF

FELIX and CALCITE

BOOK TWO, *NEVER MAKE A GIANT MAD*,
IS COMING SOON!

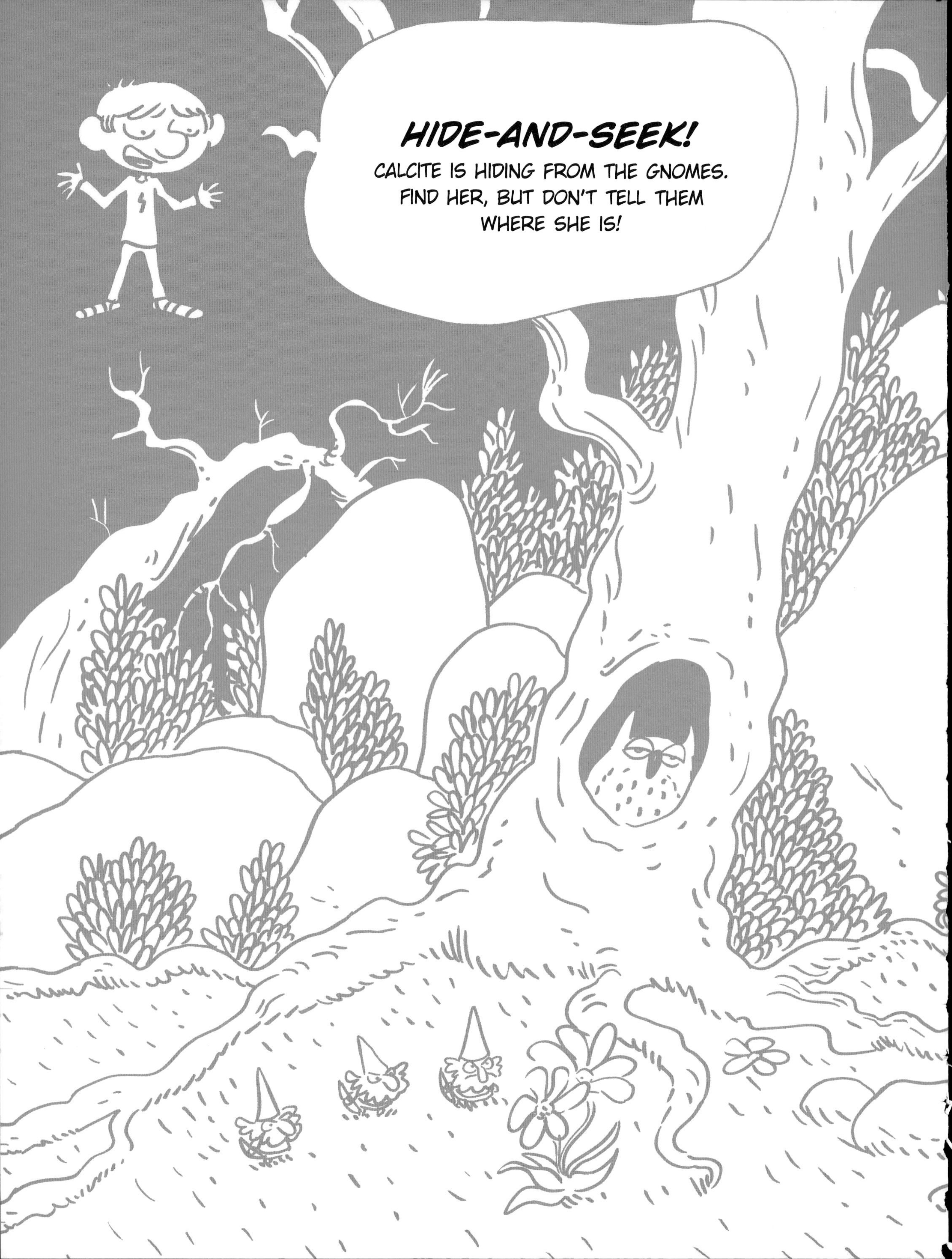
HIDE-AND-SEEK!
CALCITE IS HIDING FROM THE GNOMES. FIND HER, BUT DON'T TELL THEM WHERE SHE IS!

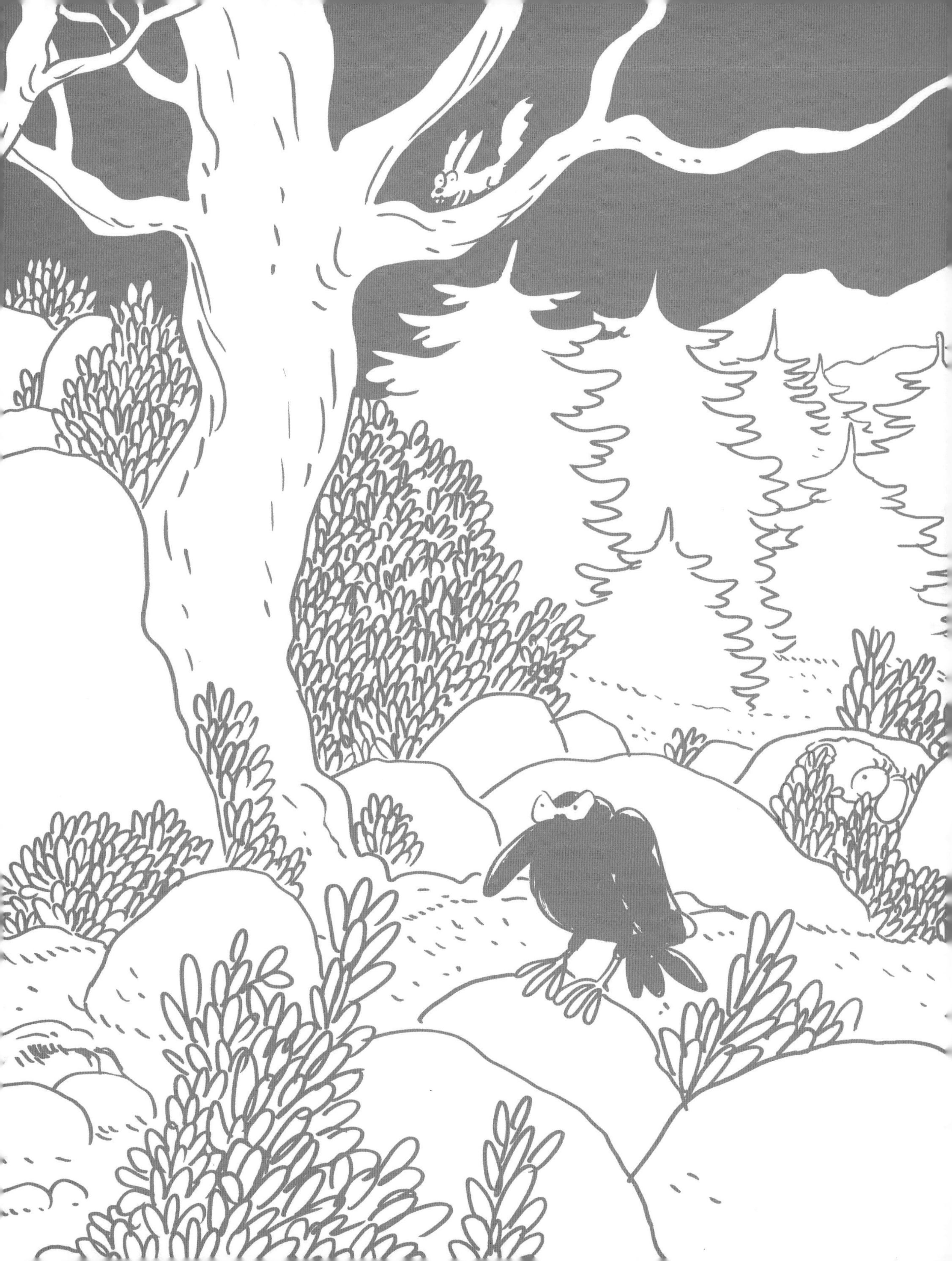

The Land of the Trolls
Story and illustrations by Artur Laperla
Translation by Norwyn MacTire

First American edition published in 2022 by Graphic Universe™

Félix y Calcita (Félix y Calcita 1) © 2020 by Penguin Random House Grupo Editorial
Travessera de Gràcia, 47-49, Barcelona 08021, Spain

Graphic Universe™ is a trademark of Lerner Publishing Group, Inc.

Graphic Universe™
An imprint of Lerner Publishing Group, Inc.
241 First Avenue North
Minneapolis, MN 55401 USA

For reading levels and more information, look up this title at www.lernerbooks.com.

Main body text set in CCWildWords. Typeface provided by Comicraft.

Library of Congress Cataloging-in-Publication Data

Names: Laperla (Artist), author, illustrator. | MacTire, Norwyn, translator.
Title: The land of the trolls / story and illustrations by Artur Laperla ; translation by Norwyn MacTire.
Description: First American edition. | Minneapolis, MN : Graphic Universe, 2022. | Series: Felix and Calcite ; book 1 | Audience: Ages 5-9 | Audience: Grades 2-3 | Summary: When Felix finds a tunnel to a land of trolls Calcite is happy to show him around, but when gnomes capture them the friendly tour looks to end early.
Identifiers: LCCN 2021018778 (print) | LCCN 2021018779 (ebook) | ISBN 9781728416328 (library binding) | ISBN 9781728448664 (paperback) | ISBN 9781728444086 (ebook)
Subjects: LCSH: Graphic novels. | CYAC: Graphic novels. | Trolls—Fiction. | Humorous stories.
Classification: LCC PZ7.7.L367 Lan 2022 (print) | LCC PZ7.7.L367 (ebook) | DDC 741.5/973—dc23

LC record available at https://lccn.loc.gov/2021018778
LC ebook record available at https://lccn.loc.gov/2021018779

Manufactured in the United States of America
1-48882-49199-7/19/2021